THE AMISH CHRISTMAS STORM

EMMA CARTWRIGHT

This is a work of fiction. Any names or characters, businesses or places, events or incidents, are fictitious. Any resemblance to actual persons, living or dead, or actual events is purely coincidental.

Copyright © 2023 by Emma Cartwright
All rights reserved.

No part of this book may be reproduced in any form or by any electronic or mechanical means, including information storage and retrieval systems, without written permission from the author, except for the use of brief quotations in a book review.
Email: emmacartwrightbooks@gmail.com

CHAPTER 1

Another chill rushed down Ruth's back and she tightened the cloak around her shoulders, wondering how her sister was managing without anything covering her lovely but thin dress against the late autumn air. Ruth could barely stand it as she stood in twice as much cloth, but Esther seemed to feel nothing at all.

"You'll catch your death," Ruth chided her younger sister again and Esther rolled her eyes, waving her away as if her words were a jinx on the festivities.

"It's my wedding, Ruthie," Esther reminded her with a happy smile, her mood unshakable. "I can bear one day of *kald*—if I could feel it at all. And we're in the *scheire* with half the district. Their body heat is spreading, and the woodstove is going. It's not so bad."

Ruth wondered if her younger sibling felt anything but the warmth of her newfound status as Eli Raber's wife. The ceremony had been long but lovely, Bishop Miller conducting a heartfelt sermon as if he wished to go out recognizably with his final wedding before spring as the Christmas season fell upon them. There was time to perform more services, but the bishop took it upon himself to host both Christmas and Old Christmas worship at his house, rendering his time limited. This would be the last wedding until the new year.

Ruth did not have a chance to argue her sister's health and comfort any further because Abigail Raber sprinted past, calling out to her smaller sister like a gust of wind, distracting them both.

"Leah!" she called in exasperation after the toddler. Seconds later, their father and Eli's brother, Joseph, hurried after both his daughters, face twisted in apology as he caught sight of his new sister-in-law and Ruth watching the scene with mild amusement.

"Forgive them," he mumbled, rushing past to secure the smaller girl, but Leah had already disappeared, leaving Abigail to give up the chase. She shook her head in annoyance, the corners of her rosebud mouth curling downward in dismay.

"She's worse than a wild *gaul*," Abigail complained.

Esther smiled patiently but cast her a nervous look. "She is still a child, Abby," she answered. "Barely older than a *bobbli*. She doesn't know what she's doing."

"She's old enough to know better," Abigail insisted, folding her arms over her chest. "If *Mamm* were here…"

Ruth's heart ached at the forlorn tone of the youngster's words, and Esther cleared her throat uncomfortably. The bride did not want talk of death ruining her day.

"I should see to Eli," she muttered, looking around for her husband.

"*Yah*," Ruth agreed. "Off you go. I'll keep Abby company."

Esther did not need to be asked again, and Ruth smiled at the seven-year-old warmly. "Have you had something to *esse?*"

Abigail studied her suspiciously, but relaxed when Ruth maintained her lovely smile.

"*Nee...Daed* is too busy chasing Leah," Abigail mumbled angrily, her arms still across her front defiantly. "He doesn't care if I'm *hungerich*."

"Then let's get you something to eat while he finds your *schweschd*er, *yah?*" Ruth offered brightly, leading the girl toward the beautiful banquet tables set up near the doors. A burst of cold air filtered past as another guest wandered through, brushing a sprinkling of multi-colored leaves along. Again, Ruth was grateful that the reception had not been held outside.

Several members of the community still lingered around the tables, laden with sweets, breads, and delicious casseroles that the women had spent days creating on Esther's behalf. There would be food to feed the Rabers until Old Christmas, for certain.

"We'll make your *vadder* something too, *yah?*" Ruth informed the girl, who continued to scowl, refusing to participate in the action of serving herself. Ruth did not inform the child that Leah was not the only one not acting her age. When Ruth had been seven, she had been cooking for her family, her own mother having lost her battle to cancer the year before. It had been Ruth's responsibility to tend to her sister while Matthew worked the farm. Abigail could not even seem to fix some food for herself.

I wonder how Joey is managing without Emma.

But Ruth also knew that the girl was still grieving the loss of her own mother and while the young girl had not acted in the same the way that Abigail had, she understood that every loss was personal. She could not judge a child for behaving the way she was.

"Will you tell me *wat* you like?" Ruth tried patiently, her cerulean eyes darting through the overflowing barn until they landed on Joseph again. He had located his youngest daughter and was crouching at her level, speaking softly to her. A smile touched Ruth's lips at the sight of his gentleness, especially when Leah began to laugh.

He certainly has a way with his daughters.

"What are you smiling at?" Abigail demanded, startling Ruth, who wrenched her eyes away guiltily.

She turned her attention back toward the food. "*Nix.*"

"You were staring at my *daed*!" Abigail insisted loudly and Ruth's cheeks went warm as she felt all the nearby eyes on her.

"I was," she agreed pleasantly, not wanting to lie to the child. "I was marveling at how patient and gentle he is with your *schweschder.*"

Ruth continued to pile glazed carrots onto the plates, casting covert glances at the frowning child whose small face only scrunched up more. Her verdant eyes looked black in her dismay, matching the shade of her hair as she stomped a foot defiantly. Ruth blinked at the gesture.

"You don't know him!" she countered furiously. "He's not patient or gentle! You're wrong about him!"

Appalled by the girl's adamance, Ruth left the matter where it was and handed her one of the plates.

"I'm not *hungerich*," Abigail declared, spinning away to storm off toward a group of other children.

She considered going after her, but changed her mind when Abigail turned around and stuck out her tongue rudely. Smothering a sigh, Ruth eyed the items in her hand and looked for Joseph instead, but her sister rejoined her as if she had been waiting for Abigail to leave.

"That *maedel*," she murmured, shaking her head. "She is spoiled rotten."

"Oh, don't say that," Ruth implored Esther. "She's had a terrible year, losing her *mudder*. It's hard on any *kin*. You don't remember because you were so small when *Mamm* died."

"*Nee*," Esther insisted. "Maybe I don't remember, but I do remember that you weren't a brat, and you were younger. Abigail was always a brat, even before Emma passed. Joseph indulges her too much."

Again, Ruth found herself looking toward the handsome, young widower, who had now picked up his smaller daughter and kept her close as he scoured the barn for his other child. He seemed to constantly be looking for one or the other, and a jab of sympathy touched her heart for him. His gaze fell on Ruth, and she waved her hands and gestured toward the group where Abigail stood. Relief crossed over Joseph's face, and he smiled gratefully at Ruth, who could not help but relish the warmth of pleasure his smile gave her.

"You really don't mind Abby?" Esther asked curiously, interest forming in her voice. Ruth flipped her attention back toward her sister.

"*Nee*. I'm sure she'll outgrow whatever this is," Ruth said confidently. "*Kinner* rarely behave badly their whole lives. I've seen enough of them to know that."

"I don't know about that..." Esther countered slowly, as if she were considering her next words carefully. "But I do know that Joseph has been talking about marrying again."

Shocked, Ruth pivoted fully, her skirt sweeping at her ankles as she did. "*Yah?*" she asked meekly, and her sister nodded, pressing a finger confidentially to her lips.

"He was telling Eli that he is feeling lost without a *frau* in his *haus*," she whispered, leaning in. "And I think that all this talk of our wedding has him thinking about it."

Ruth nodded slowly, turning back to the man across the floor. His profile was evident. His thick, auburn beard could be seen through the throng of well-wishers, his hat pulled down over his sweeping hair. If he turned just slightly, Ruth would be able to make out his vivid, emerald eyes that always seemed slightly sad, even before his wife had passed.

"He has been struggling a great deal," Esther went on in a very low voice. "He wouldn't want anyone to know about this, Ruthie. *Pliese*, don't breath any of it—to anyone."

"I wouldn't say a word," Ruth vowed, and Esther squeezed her arm softly.

"I know or I wouldn't tell you."

The sisters exchanged a glance.

"Would you be interested in spending some time with him?" Esther asked after a moment of silence. "We could set it up, maybe?"

"Very much," Ruth answered without hesitation. She blushed at her unabashed answer, but she would be remiss if she did not admit her admiration for the shopkeeper.

"And you don't mind that he has the two *maedel?*" Esther pressed worriedly. Her sister seemed more concerned about the children than Ruth.

"I like *kinner*, Essie. You know that. I'm a midwife!" Ruth chided lightly.

Esther sniggered.

"I know, but…" Esther sighed and then brightened. "It would be something if we ended up marrying *bruders, yah?*"

Instantly, Ruth looked toward her father, who was staring at his two daughters, his brow furrowed as if he could sense the seriousness of their conversation. Matthew Bieler cocked his head to the side in question, and Ruth's blush deepened further.

Why does it always seem like he knows what we're saying?

"You won't say anything to *Daed*, will you?" she asked Esther.

"*Nee*, no one," Esther promised. "We'll see how this works out first."

Ruth nodded, her shoulders relaxing. "Then *yah*, you can tell Joseph I would be willing to court him."

Esther giggled. "After today," she reminded Ruth, as though anyone could possibly forget that it was her wedding day.

"After today," Ruth conceded.

"*Gut.*" Esther flittered off again to attend to her guests and Matthew ambled to up to his eldest daughter.

"*Wat* were you and your *schweschder* talking so intently about?" her father asked.

"Many things," Ruth answered evasively, willing away the crimson of her cheeks. "*Chrischdaag*, Eli…your retirement."

Matthew frowned deeply. "Enough of that!" he grumbled sullenly, his hand touching his leg subconsciously. "I won't have you two gossiping about me, just like the rest of this town."

"No one gossips about you, *Daed*," Ruth reassured him. "We're all concerned about you since you were hurt in the accident—"

"It was barely an accident!" he interjected. "I wish you'd stop calling it an accident."

"It was an accident enough that you weren't able to work for a month," Ruth reminded him dryly, but *she* wished she had not brought the subject up. Her hope had been to steer him away from asking about her and Esther's conversation, not upset him.

"It hasn't affected the harvest in the least," Matthew added.

Ruth did not remind him that was because she and Esther had been working twice as hard to ensure that all the work was done. But with Esther leaving for the Raber house, next year would be much more difficult and Ruth did not want to think about it.

Unless Joseph Raber comes to our farm to hilf…

Ruth's flush returned to her cheeks, and she silently chided herself for getting ahead of herself.

"Nevermind all that today," Ruth told him, taking his arm and guiding him toward the food table. "Today is about Esther and Eli, *nix* else."

Matthew grumbled something incoherent, but he did not protest as his daughter fixed him a small plate of butter tarts and frosted cakes. It was far too festive a day for bad moods, and Christmas would soon be upon them.

And perhaps another wedding for next year, if Ruth was lucky.

CHAPTER 2

There had been a short time after his wife had passed when Joseph Raber had believed he would succeed without her. The neighbors and his family paid him regular visits, the women loading the household with food and cleaning in their wake, tending to the girls and picking up where Emma had left off. They had given him the illusion that he could carry on as if everything would continue as normal.

But when the period of mourning had passed, their attendance diminished, leaving Joseph with the harsh reality that he was a single father at younger than thirty and his daughters had no mother to learn the most basic of tasks from in their formative years.

He began to see where he and Emma had failed Abigail, treating her too delicately, doing too much for her. The girl could not do the simplest of tasks to assist in running the house, and Joseph was in no position to help her learn.

It had been his brother, Eli, who had first roused the idea of remarrying and Joseph had been staunchly against it from the start.

"Emma hasn't even been gone a year," he reminded his younger brother, who nodded in agreement.

"It will be your first *Chrischdaag* without her," Eli conceded. "Think of what that will mean for the *maedel*. They will not handle the change well. It's better to have someone there for *Chrischdaag*, I think."

At first, Joseph had dismissed the idea, the thought of bringing a new woman into his life so soon was strange. He had loved Emma as a husband should, and her loss had left a void in him. While he was not opposed to the idea of finding another wife, if only to ensure his daughters had a mother, the thought of marrying so quickly did not sit well with him.

But as the spring had turned to summer and summer to fall, his life began to disintegrate, day by day. With the juggle of keeping his wayward Leah from slipping out of his caregiver's watch and manning Abigail's increasingly sullen moods while attending to his store, Joseph quickly realized just how difficult things were.

His family did their best to keep up with his family's needs, but the truth was becoming blindingly clear. It was not the support of relatives that he needed: Joseph desperately needed a wife. Eli had been entirely right.

The discussion had been an embarrassing one when he had raised it with his brother a few days before the wedding.

"I've given a lot of thought to what we discussed and I believe you're right," he informed Eli. "I believe I have to remarry."

Eli had not been surprised by his brother's revelation, but he had warned him of the timing.

"*Chrischdaag* is upon us, Joe, and there are not many *frau* in Benny's Creek. I wish you'd come to your senses a little earlier."

None of this was news to Joseph. He was well aware of both facts, the community still relatively new, despite their Old Order manner of doing things. Despite their endless attempts to recruit new members to their small spot near the Cheney Reservoir, their numbers were still quite low.

"Maybe after *Chrischdaag*, we can go to Anderson County," Eli suggested. "Or even out of state and find someone to bring here."

Joseph had agreed at the time, swallowing his protests that it would be too long to wait. He was already hanging on by a thread. But there was nothing that his brother could do about it, his own wedding on the horizon, and Joseph did not wish to take away from Eli's own happiness by presenting his problems.

Joseph continued to suffer in silence. He was reminded of his loss, his daughters' loss, each day as Christmas drew closer, the shoppers in his store wanting to know what supplies he had so that they could consider what presents they hoped to give their loved ones over the festive season. The hours in the small craft shop he had started now seemed unbearable and what had once been his pride and joy suddenly felt like a prison.

Maybe I should sell the shop and go back to warrick in the factory. It would mean steadier hours for the maedel and less interaction with the community.

But it would also mean depending on the community to raise his two lost daughters as he worked long hours away from home. It was the reason he had given up working at the cannery in the first place.

No solution seemed to fit now that Emma was gone. All the answers seemed as if they were the wrong ones.

The day after the wedding, Eli appeared in the shop, startling Joseph.

"Aren't you supposed to be on your *bossdaage*?" the older brother demanded, blinking worriedly as he slid around the side of the counter to greet Eli. "Has something happened? Is Esther all right?"

"*Yah*, everything is fine." Eli chuckled. "We're leaving later this afternoon."

"Oh…" Confused, he cocked his head. "*Wat* are you doing here then? Shouldn't you be packing and getting ready to leave?"

Eli chuckled and clapped his brother on the shoulder. "Are you trying to get rid of me?" he teased.

"*Nee*, of course not. I like having you here, but I think your bride expects a honeymoon and you wouldn't want to start your marriage off with an unhappy bride. I know that much."

"Esther will get her honeymoon," Eli promised. "But I wanted to talk to you before I left. She told me something that might be of interest to you and I thought you should hear about it before I go. It shouldn't wait."

Joseph raised an eyebrow, perplexed by the mystery enshrouding his brother. "*Wat* is it?"

"Ruthie Bieler," he announced, a smile forming on his clean-shaven face, his green eyes brightening as if he had said something earth changing. But it meant nothing to Joseph.

"Esther's *schweschder*? The midwife?" Joseph asked, more confusion overtaking him. "*Wat* about her?"

"*Wat* do you think of her?"

Joseph scratched his reddish beard and pursed his lips, thinking about the little that he knew about the stately, blue-eyed sister of his sister-in-law. He knew very little about her.

Ruth had delivered Leah and, while Joseph had been grateful for her help, the woman had always struck him as more of one of Matthew's sons than daughters. Perhaps it was her height or her slightly peculiar nature that had made him think that way.

"She's very pleasant…" Joseph offered, unsure of what else he was being asked. "She delivered Leah and Emma liked her well enough."

"*Yah*," Eli agreed with a vehement nod. "And she's not so *auld* yet. She's twenty-six."

Suddenly, Joseph understood what Eli was proposing. "Oh!"

He blinked several times, considering the tall, blonde woman in a different light. She was attractive, although not in the same way as her younger sister. Ruth was less effeminate, more…determined, serious.

"I didn't think she was interested in anything but the *familye* farm and delivering *bobbli*," Joseph confessed.

"Neither did I," Eli admitted. "But Esther assures me that she's taken an interest in you, too."

Unsure of what to make of this newfound revelation, Joseph stared at his hands as Eli chuckled dryly. "I know it wasn't what you were expecting and I can say *nee—*"

"*Nee*," he interjected, thinking of the alternative. If he rejected this offer, it would mean waiting weeks for Eli to return, for Old Christmas to pass, and hope that the snow didn't block the roads for them to travel out of the district. "*Nee*, she is a *gut frau*. She is honest and hard-working. I saw her with Abby *geschder*. She is patient with *kinner*. She's a *gut* fit."

"She does *warrick* very hard," Eli agreed, although he sounded worried. "She and Esther have put in a lot of extra time at the farm since Matthew's accident. I don't know how much longer they can expect to keep that up."

Joseph frowned, unsure of how that would tie into any future plans of his.

"But that isn't your concern right now," Eli added, as if reading his brother's thoughts. "I'll let Ruthie know that you are open to speaking with her after *Chrischdaag—*"

"*NEE!*" Joseph choked. He was sure he could not wait until after Christmas to move things along. It was the whole point of agreeing to meet with Ruth in the first place.

Eli blinked. "*Nee?*"

Joseph shook his head. "Have her *komme* by today, if Esther sees her before you leave. If not..."

He thought about how he might manage to swing by the Bieler property before heading home to his daughters.

"Okay," Eli conceded. "We'll let her know before."

Relieved, Joseph offered his brother a smile and nodded. "Have a *gut* week and enjoy yourselves. I'll see you when you return."

"You take care of yourself, *yah*?" Eli said worriedly. "Make sure you use the neighbors and the *kossin* when we're gone. Try not to let *Mamm* and *Daed* drive you *narricht*."

"It's a little late for that," Joseph sighed dryly.

"I'm serious, Joey. Don't be ashamed to ask for *hilf* and don't let *Mamm* and *Daed* shame you with their lectures."

"We'll manage," Joseph told him firmly, although he was not sure that was the truth. With their parents getting older, Joseph loathed to ask for their help with his daughters, especially the rambunctious Leah. He knew his parents were likely to suggest all sorts of archaic parenting that he could not abide.

"Until next week," Joseph said, ushering his younger sibling out of the cozy store. With a backward glance, Eli hurried out of the shop and toward his waiting buggy as Joseph waved him off.

Then he turned back to deal with the rest of his insurmountable day.

Joseph might have forgotten the entire conversation with Eli, with the bustle of business he had over the next few hours. Members of the community flocked through his doors, fingering the woodcarvings he had spent painstaking hours making in the woodshop at his house. His aunt's woven baskets sold fast, and he made notes to have her restock for the upcoming weeks, his cousin's quilts selling just as quickly to the Englishers who wandered through.

His was one of the few year-round shops that remained in Benny's Creek, the other Amish shops only keeping open for market days. Joseph took great pride in his pieces, the family craftwork that had been passed down for generations.

"*Daed*! *Mammi* is tired of watching Leah again!"

Abigail's voice rang across the shop as Joseph wrapped up his latest sale and he saw his mother amble through the door tiredly, Leah on her hand firmly as his older daughter marched forward.

"*Denki*," he mumbled at the customer, turning his attention toward his mother and daughters. His heart dropped to see them.

Is she going to leave them in the shop again?

It would not be the first time his mother had done that, merely to teach the girls a lesson.

"That's not true," Liza Raber said and sighed, casting Abigail a reproving stare. "Leah wanted to see you."

Eagerly, the smaller girl extended her arms toward her father as the bell dinged over the entrance of the shop again as Joseph reached for his youngest.

Picking up his daughter, he turned to greet the latest customer and gasped aloud to see Ruth Bieler with a platter in her mitted hands, blue eyes blinking nervously to see his family in front of him.

Oh no...the timing is terrible.

But he could not very well turn her away.

She offered him a timid smile, but the discomfort on her face was palpable.

"Oh, *hallo*..." Joseph mumbled.

"*H-hallo*," she sputtered, glancing back toward the door as if she were considering bolting back out the way she had come. "I-I brought some *eepies* for you and the *maedel*."

She lifted the covered plate in her hands and Leah squeaked happily. "*EEPIE!*"

Liza eyed Ruth with interest as the woman shuffled forward to place the cookies onto the counter and Joseph cleared his throat. "*Denki*, Ruth. Say *hallo* to Ruth, Abby."

Abigail cast her a sidelong look before removing the cover and peering at the baked goodies underneath. "*Hallo*," she mumbled, snatching up a cookie. Leah grabbed for one also and Joseph set the little girl back on the ground as Liza rounded the girls away from the counter, sensing their need to speak in private.

"*Es dutt mer leed*," Ruth apologized the moment they were out of earshot. "I-I didn't realize that everyone was here."

"You have nothing to be sorry for," Joseph reassured her. "That's very kind of you. *Denki*, for thinking of us."

He offered her a timid smile, and she returned it, relief falling over her face. "Eli spoke to you, did he?"

Joseph nodded and Ruth blushed lightly. "I know you're very *bissi*," she rushed on. "And I won't keep you. I only wanted..."

She trailed off and looked at the ground, pursing her lips together. "I wanted to bring you some cookies."

Joseph chuckled lightly. "They've been received very well," he said, nodding toward the children who had already devoured their treats. Abigail raised her dark head of hair to peer speculatively at the pair, and Joseph smiled at her.

"Can I have another, *Daed*?" she asked from across the store.

"Ask Ruthie," he instructed. She turned her vivid green eyes on Ruth and gave the woman an enchanting beam.

"*Pliese*, Ruthie?"

"Don't *esse* too many," Liza warned quickly. "You'll ruin your *nachtesse*."

Ruth flushed crimson, but Joseph gave his mother a warning look, which she immediately understood. "One more and a promise that you'll *esse* your *nachtesse, yah*?"

On a whim, he blurted out. "You'll join us for *nachtesse dienacht*, Ruthie?"

The air in the shop shifted as Abigail froze mid-step and Ruth gawked at the unexpected invitation.

"I…*yah, denki*," she mumbled, clearly taken aback by the offer. "*Wat* can I bring?"

Joseph looked at his mother, who also looked stunned by the turn of events, but Liza recovered quickly. "Ask your *vadder* if he would like to join us also," Liza suggested. "You don't need to bring anything. It will be simple."

Abigail appeared to change her mind about the cookies and spun around, storming toward the back room, slamming the door behind her.

"That *maedel*," Liza grumbled at Joseph. "You need to do something about her, Joey."

He exhaled and hung his head, but before he could respond, the door opened yet again and he was forced to deal with the new throng of customers entering.

"I could talk to her," Ruth offered. "We got along well enough at the wedding."

Joseph did not protest, but he did not have high hopes for her success. Abigail's terrible attitude was only increasing over time.

"I will see you *dienacht*," he told her, hurrying to tend to the newcomers as she took the platter of cookies toward the back room, hoping to coax Abigail out.

But when Joseph had finally finished with the next round of sales, his eldest daughter was still in the backroom, refusing to come out and Ruth was gone, the cookies on a side table near the door.

"*Wat* happened?" Joseph asked, his brow furrowed as he looked about for Ruth. Liza shrugged and shook her head.

"Abby happened," she informed him haughtily. "She was rude to Ruthie."

"Why?" Joseph asked, dumbfounded. Liza grimaced, glancing at her smaller granddaughter, who had wandered off to play with one of the whittled figures in a corner.

"If I had to guess, Joey, I would assume she doesn't like the idea of Ruth Bieler *cooma* around here."

Joseph's grimace deepened, but he was not surprised. Abigail was happy with so little these days. Courting another woman was bound to be met with some resistance by Abigail.

"It's for the best," Joseph mumbled, more to himself than to his mother. He was still not sure if he was convincing himself or the others.

CHAPTER 3

*J*oseph considered canceling supper that night when he could not get Abigail to speak sensibly with him beforehand.

"I don't know what to do with her," he said with a long sigh.

"You won't let a *kin* dictate how to proceed in adult affairs," Liza told him flatly. "You're doing what's best for all of you. But I have to admit, Joey, I am surprised. Ruthie Bieler?"

Joseph gave her a wary stare. "What's wrong with Ruth Bieler?" he asked her, a defensiveness unexpectedly enveloping him.

"*Nix*! She's lovely. I'm shocked she's interested in marriage. Matthew must be doing better if she's entertaining it. She's been very committed to helping him with the farm and her *warrick* and helping him keep the house clean." Liza leaned in over the kitchen counter and lowered her voice. "Have you been courting her long?"

Joseph felt as though his cheeks were on fire and he turned his head away, grateful for the whiskers on his face covering his hot blush. He ran his fingers through his beard, purposely keeping his cheeks turned away from his mother's pointed stare.

"We haven't even started," he admitted.

"Really?" Liza sounded amused. "The way you were making eyes at one another in the shop—"

Abigail wandered into the kitchen and the pair abruptly stopped speaking.

"Abby, Ruthie Bieler is *cooma* for *nachtesse*. I expect you to be on your best behavior *dienacht*," Joseph told her sternly. "I won't tolerate anymore of this storming off and sulking like you've been—"

"*Nee!*" she interjected, her face brightening in defiance. "Nobody said she could *komme!*"

Joseph bristled, but Liza smoothly interjected. "Our doors are always open to *familye*, Abby. She's your *onkle's weib's schweschder*," Liza reminded her.

"Eli and Esther aren't here!" Abigail insisted.

"That doesn't matter." Joseph frowned, sweat breaking out over his brow. His courtship with Ruth hadn't even begun, and they were already facing troubles.

"If she is coming, I'm not coming down from my room!" Abigail threatened, crossing her arms over her chest.

Joseph parted his lips to respond, but his mother spoke first. "*Gut*. Then you'll go to bed without *nachtesse*. In fact, you can go now. Off you go. Don't *komme* out until *mariye*."

Dumbfounded, Abigail looked from her father to grandmother, but Liza extended her finger insistently. "I won't tell you again."

Joseph's heart ached at the punishment, but he did not undermine his mother's orders as Abigail burst into tears and fled for her bedroom.

"*Mamm...*" Joseph sighed.

"You need to stop coddling her," Liza insisted. "I know you are giving her *leeway* because of her grief, but she will only get worse. She is already getting worse."

Joseph inhaled deeply and nodded, lowering his gaze. He did not agree with Liza's harsh techniques, but he could not deny that his mother had a point. His gentle parenting was not improving Abigail's surliness.

And how will Ruth feel about this?

"Maybe it is for the best if she sits this *nachtesse* out," Joseph agreed with a heavy sigh. "We'll prepare her better for the next one."

Ruth fit into Joseph's life seamlessly. She did not demand a lot and found ways to make his days easier.

While he was at the shop, she brought him meals in huge picnic baskets, filled to the brim, the sight of them making him laugh every time.

"How much *esse* could I possibly eat before *nachtesse* every day?" he had teased her the first time he had seen it, but Ruth only laughed and revealed the inside of the basket. It was not just a tasty assortment of sandwiches and cheese to get him through the long day, but thick boughs of holly and candles to decorate his shop for the upcoming holiday.

"I thought that it could use a touch of green in here," she admitted. "I hope you don't mind. All the other shops in town have decorations. Yours seems so empty."

Joseph's smile faded. "I haven't felt much like putting anything up this year," he confessed.

Ruth nodded understandingly. "I don't mean to push the idea on you, but I thought it might *hilf* the girls. It could lift Abby's spirits?"

She did not sound convinced, but Joseph appreciated her trying at all. He had not thought about much in the way of Christmas, beyond what kind of pain it would bring to the household.

"I like the idea very much," he told her honestly. "I hope you will *hilf* me put them up."

Her face glowed, and she agreed—with a condition.

"You will have to bring the *maedel* to my *haus* and *hilf* me and my *vadder* put up ours. Without Esther there now, I have so much *warrick* to do."

She eyed him uncertainly, as if she was worried he might refuse, but Joseph nodded emphatically. "I think that's a fine idea," he replied. A change of scenery would do them all good.

Ruth continued to fill the huge picnic basket with decorations and lunch and on Friday night, he gathered his daughters for dinner and decorating at the Beilers.

"I don't want to go!" Abigail grouched as he ushered her onto the buggy, her breath escaping into the night air in puffs. Joseph slipped against the icy ground, catching himself before he could fall, and Leah giggled at the spectacle.

"Into the *waegel*, *pliese*," Joseph said sternly.

"*Nee*! I don't want to!" Abigail screeched. Joseph stopped and glowered at his older daughter, his patience expiring entirely.

"That's enough out of you, Abby!" he snapped. "I won't hear another word. If you continue to behave this badly, I will…" He wracked his brain for a punishment that his mother might use but stopped himself. "You'll behave."

Pouting, Abigail climbed into the cab and pulled her little sister onto her lap, grabbing a thick woolen blanket to warm themselves.

Sighing, Joseph pulled himself up and took the reins, hoping he had heard the last of Abigail's griping for the night.

The latest snowfall had made the country roads slightly treacherous, and he led the horses gently across the district until they were upon the Bieler's thriving soybean farm.

Promise of winter had quieted the potential that the fields showed throughout the rest of the year, but Joseph hardly had a chance to notice any of that with Abigail's incessant complaining from the back of the buggy.

"I don't want to be here, *Daed*," she howled.

"If you don't have anything kind to share, Abby, *pliese* don't bother speaking *dienacht*," Joseph warned her as they dismounted the cart, his strong arms collecting Leah so that she did not slide over the snowy walkway.

"Oh," Ruth called out from the doorway, hurrying forward to greet them, her head hung in shame. "I did mean to salt that before you arrived."

With a final warning look at his eldest, Joseph smiled at Ruth.

"We've seen worse, haven't we?" he joked, bouncing Leah on his hip, and the girl giggled, extending her arms toward Ruth. Abigail was aghast by her sister's display and stormed toward the front of the house without a word as Ruth looked on.

"Is she all right?" Ruth asked worriedly.

"She will be," Joseph said firmly, but he was unsure he spoke the truth. He prayed that his daughter would accept his choices and embrace Ruth, but he could not force the woman upon her.

Matthew joined them in the living room, helping as Ruth instructed the men where to hang the garlands over the curtain rods, as Leah gleefully added to the festivities by pointing out her own opinions.

"I think there's another box in the basement," Ruth informed them when the final touches were put on the Bieler household and all the cider was consumed. "I promise, it's the last."

"I'll get it," Matthew offered, but Ruth insisted that her father sit in the living room with Joseph and the girls.

"Would you like to *komme* with me, Abby?" she offered the quiet older girl.

"Into the creepy cellar?" Abigail retorted sharply. "*Nee, denki.*"

"Abby!" Joseph cried sharply, but Ruth shook her head. "It's all right. I don't blame her."

Smiling, she excused herself and headed into the basement, leaving Joseph to frown at Abigail. He wagged a finger sternly. "I warned you."

"Did you warn me about replacing *Mamm*?" she fired back. "Not even a year after she was taken to *Gott*?"

Joseph paled, and he looked nervously at Matthew, who started to shake his head.

"Abby, that's not true." Joseph sighed.

"It is true! It is! *Wat* else are we doing here if not that?!"

"*Liebling—*" Matthew leaned forward to help, but Abigail only scowled at him.

"You don't know me!" she cried, her voice raising to a familiar pitch that Joseph knew all too well.

Leah's head cocked up from where she was playing, her own bright eyes filling with pain to hear her sister's cries.

"You're right," Matthew agreed quickly. "But I'd like to."

"*Nee!*" Abigail cried. "You only want to marry off your *auld dochder* to my *daed*!"

Matthew's eyes widened as he met Joseph's humiliated stare.

"Abigail, that's not—"

"It is!" Abigail shrieked, her raised voice agitating her sister, who began to wail.

"Abby!" Joseph tried to intercede, but it was pointless now with both of his daughters crying. Abigail jumped up from her spot on the stairs and rushed toward the second floor as Leah began to sob, calling after her sister. Helplessly, Joseph moved to comfort the younger girl as Ruth returned from the basement, her face twisted in confusion.

"*Wat* is going on?" Ruth demanded, setting down the box in her hand. "*Wat* happened?"

"*Nix*—" Joseph started to say, but Matthew felt no need to lie to his daughter and told her exactly what the fuss was all about.

"*Yung* Abigail seems to think that her *vadder* is trying to replace her *mudder*." Matthew sighed, reclaiming his place in his wing chair, shaking his graying head.

Joseph wrapped Leah in his arms, shushing her until her crying subsided and cast Ruth an apologetic look, but she appeared aghast by the revelation.

"*Wat?*" she gasped. "She said that?"

"She is *yung*…" Joseph offered lamely, and Ruth exhaled.

"I wish you would have told me that she was taking this so badly," she informed him sadly. Joseph's jaw twitched.

"Only time will heal her pain, Ruthie. She is too young to explain it to her," he muttered. Ruth pursed her lips, her eyes traveling toward the second floor, but she nodded slowly.

"I understand why she's been so rude to me now," she mumbled.

"I won't let her do that anymore," Joseph tried to say, but Ruth shook her blonde braid again.

"This isn't Abby's fault," she insisted. "The child is missing her *mudder*. No one is going to be worthy of replacing Emma—not that I would ever want to do that."

She bit on her lower lip, again looking up the stairs as if she were considering going after the seven-year-old.

"I have to show her that I have no interest in doing that," she murmured, the thought spoken aloud.

"We will work this out," Joseph promised quickly, but Ruth put her hand on his arm.

"This is between me and Abigail," she said softly. "I have to show the *maedel* that I am not a threat to your *familye*."

Joseph admired her optimism, but he was not sure that Abigail would be so easily swayed.

"I won't stand in your way if you want to try," he agreed softly. "But I'm afraid you might have your *warrick* cut out."

"*Gott* will see us through this," Abigail said firmly. "He always does."

CHAPTER 4

The festive spirit quickly expired after Abigail's outburst and with apologies springing from his lips, Joseph rounded up his children to bring them home.

"You will be punished for your behavior, *dienacht*," Joseph warned his eldest daughter. To his surprise, Abigail did not respond. Her head turned defiantly away from him as she looked out toward the frosted landscape instead. "Did you hear me, Abby?"

"I hear you, *Daed*!" Leah chirped for her sister, but Joseph did not smile. His hands tightened around the reins, and he urged the horses to move faster, the chill of the night getting under his skin now. His agitation with Abigail was mounting, and he did not know what to do with his eldest daughter anymore. He feared that her temperament would scare off Ruth, the only woman in the community who had shown any real interest in him since Emma had passed.

He maintained his silence for the rest of the way home, but when he arrived, he was shocked to find his brother's buggy waiting.

"There you are!" Eli called from the porch where he sat, drinking a hot cider. Esther sat in the neighboring seat. Abigail rushed off into the house and Joseph paused for a moment as Leah rushed toward Esther.

"You're back already?" Joseph asked, his gaze trailing after his daughter.

"It's been a week." Esther chuckled. "You didn't miss us much, I hear."

Joseph exhaled. "Will you keep an eye on Leah? I have to speak with Abby."

Eli's smile faded, but he nodded in agreement as his older brother retreated into the fire-warmed house after his child. He found Abigail in her room, crying softly, and his earlier anger dissipated.

"Abby..." He sighed, closing the door so that they wouldn't be interrupted. "*Nee*, Abby, don't cry."

"I'm crying for *Mamm*!" she mumbled in a shuddering breath. "Since no one else remembers her!"

Joseph perched on the edge of her bed and shook his head passionately. "That's just not true, Abby. I think about your *mudder* every day."

Abigail scoffed as if she did not believe him, but he reached for her small hand and forced her to look at him. "I do. And I miss her all the time. She was a *gut frau* and a good *mudder* to you and your *schweschder*. We were lucky to have her. *Gott* took her too soon, but *pliese* believe me when I say I loved her with all my heart."

Abigail swallowed, drying her eyes with her free hand. "If you miss her, you wouldn't be trying to replace her," she insisted.

"No one could ever replace your *mudder*, Abby. That's not what Ruthie is trying to do."

"Are you saying you're not going to marry her?" Abigail grumbled, pulling her hand back.

"*Nee*," Joseph replied honestly. "That's not what I'm saying. But that doesn't mean I am trying to replace your *mudder*."

"Then why would you marry someone so soon after she's gone! It hasn't been a year!"

Joseph had to remind himself how young his child was, how much she did not understand about the world.

Perhaps it's time to make her see now.

"Abigail, you and your *schweschder* need a *mudder*—" he immediately cringed at his wording and quickly spoke over himself. "You need extra care, care that I can't give you when I have the shop to run and products to make."

"We have a *mudder*," Abigail answered predictably.

"Not one who will teach you to *koche* and clean and sew."

"We have *Grossmammi*!"

"Abigail, *Grossmammi* is *auld*," Joseph said bluntly. "She can't keep up with you. You've seen how many times she brings you to the shop when she's minding you. It's too much to ask of her."

"Esther!" Abigail suggested frantically. "We have neighbors and *freind*—"

"Abby, it's not their responsibility. It's mine. And my decision, not yours." He inhaled, steeling himself from getting angry again. He did not want to turn this conversation into another fight.

"It's disrespectful to *Mamm's* memory!" she insisted, becoming agitated again.

"It's *Gott's* will!" Joseph replied firmly. "He wants you and your *schweshder* to have a *mudder*. He wants all *mann* to have a *weib*. You are not thinking with your head, only your heart."

"You're heartless!" she spat, and Joseph recoiled at the insult.

"Abby…"

"Leave me alone!"

"Abby…"

She turned around and faced the wall, curling into a ball, leaving Joseph with little choice but to respect her wishes. Sighing deeply, he rose from his place and withdrew to the main floor where his mother and father had retreated to the front room with Leah and the newlyweds.

"*Wat* is wrong with her now?" Liza grumbled.

"*Nix*," Joseph said quickly, certain that his mother would only go up and make things worse if he told her. "Eli, will you *hilf* me outside. I need to get more wood."

Immediately, his brother rose, Esther casting them both worried looks, but Joseph cast her a warm smile. "Your *schweschder* is *wunderbar*."

Relief sank into Esther's shoulders as she recognized that her suspicions were unfounded, and she sank back into the sofa, gesturing for Leah to climb into her lap. "*Gut.* I'm glad things are working out," she said happily.

But when they were outside, Joseph abruptly turned to his brother and threw up his hands. "I don't know what to do!" he exclaimed. Concern overtook Eli's face, and the younger brother looked back toward the house.

"Things aren't going well with Ruthie?" he mumbled worriedly.

"*Nee, nee.* Ruthie truly is *wunderbar*. Leah adores her and I…" Joseph cleared his throat nervously before he could reveal too much about his innermost feelings. He was conflicted about the unexpected tenderness he felt toward Esther's sister.

But maybe none of that will matter if things continue as they are with Abigail.

"Abby resents her," Joseph explained as his brother stared at him expectantly. "She accused me of replacing Emma."

"Ah…" Eli nodded sagely. "I suppose that was to be expected."

"She is old enough to understand the way of things, isn't she?" Joseph asked, placing his hands on the rail of the porch to peer out into the night. He wondered what Ruth would be doing in that moment now that their evening had been cut short.

Will she still komme to the shop again tomorrow or will she decide that it's all too much now?

He posed the question aloud to Eli.

To his surprise, Eli chuckled. "You don't know Ruthie very well if you think she would just give up because of a child's *yess*. She's strong, remember? She knows all about *kinner*. All kinds of *kinner*."

"But this is different," the older man insisted. "This is personal, and Abigail is making it very difficult for her. She didn't agree to any of this."

"Abigail will learn to accept Ruthie. She's a *gut*, kind *frau* who will win your wayward *maedel* over whether Abby likes it or not. You just have to give it time."

But Joseph was not sure that they had the luxury of time, not when Abigail was making things so complicated.

"I'll talk to Ruthie," a small, feminine voice offered from behind them. "And explain your dilemma."

Joseph spun around, humiliation coloring his face as he realized Esther had overheard every word they had spoken. "Essie, I—"

"Eli is right," she told him gently, a warm smile overtaking her face. "Ruthie isn't likely to give up so easily, but I'll let her know that you aren't giving up either, and that you want to pursue what you have together."

Joseph met her sweet blue eyes and exhaled. "I don't foresee this getting any better."

"Ruthie will find a way," Esther said confidently. "She has a way with *kinner*."

Joseph wished he shared in her optimism, but it was difficult when Abigail would not listen to reason.

She misses her mudder too much and short of bringing Emma back from Gott's embrace, I don't know how else to please that girl.

CHAPTER 5

*E*sther worked tirelessly with her sister to prepare gifts for the children for Christmas Day.

"You should be *deheem* preparing for your first *Chrischdaag* with your *mann*," Ruth told her sibling apologetically.

"Don't be silly." Esther chuckled. "Liza has all the plans just so, and she doesn't want me in the way. Anyway, she makes a much bigger fuss over Old *Chrischdaag* than this one."

She was thankful that she had the extra help. For the past week, she had gone out of her way to plan special gifts for Leah and Abigail, hoping to win the older girl over in the wake of what had happened.

Although Abigail did not have outbursts in front of Ruth, her animus was palpable, and the young woman was sure she only held her tongue because she feared her father's punishment. That was not the relationship she wanted to have with Abigail, but she seemed to be getting nowhere on her own.

"I don't know what the Bishop would say about buying her affections," Esther told Ruth and the older sister blushed.

"*Wat?*" she demanded. "I'm not buying anything! Everything is made out of *lieb!*"

"You know what I mean," Esther insisted, staring steadfastly at Ruth. "You're going to so much trouble to win this girl over, but she has no respect for you whatsoever. You shouldn't try to win her love through material gain."

"I'm not!" Ruth insisted hotly, but the harder Esther looked at her, the more Ruth blushed.

She finally threw up her hands. "I don't know what else to do, Essie! She really does think I've *komme* to steal her *vadder*."

"She is a child, Ruthie. It doesn't matter what you say to her, she won't understand it. Bishop Miller has tried speaking with her and while she's not as rude to him, *denki* goodness, it's clear she's not listening to him either."

Ruth stifled a sigh and continued her careful stitching of the doll in her hand. She had made two, identical for each of Joseph's children, putting extra love and care into each. She knew that her sister was right about "buying" Abigail's affections, but she was out of ideas.

Usually, Christmas was a wonderous time for her, despite the fact that she and Esther had also lost their mother at a young age. Matthew had helped his daughters to overcome the heartbreak of such a tragedy and they had prevailed. Ruth hoped to show Abigail that it was possible.

Of course, Daed never tried to bring another frau deheem so soon after Mamm passed. Maybe I would have felt strongly about that too.

It was difficult to predict just how she or Esther would have reacted to Matthew bringing home another wife, but Ruth liked to think she would have handled the matter better than Abigail. She could also see now that Abigail's issues had started far before Emma's death. Perhaps Joseph had coddled her and Leah too much with his kindness, creating something of an overindulged child in the end. Abigail was nowhere proficient in the same traits that Ruth had known at seven, from cooking to sewing or even basic cleaning.

It will be my job to teach her all that too, Ruth thought, and she was not sure she could manage it. Abigail already disliked her enough.

"Where have you gone now?" Esther demanded, willing her sister back to the present. Ruth gave her a quick grin and shook her blonde mane hastily.

"Nowhere," she promised. "I'm here with you."

"I won't let that *maedel* ruin our *Chrischdaag*," Esther insisted firmly. "Liza won't stand for it, either."

Ruth grimaced at the notion of Liza overtaking Abigail's punishment.

"I'm sure she'll come around," Ruth offered weakly. But she already knew then that her prophecy was a poor one.

On Christmas Eve, Joseph and the girls went over to the Bielers to have a meal which Ruth had spent all day making. She had also gone out of her way to find more décor to liven up the household, adding pretty garlands on the exterior to greet the girls when they drove up.

Leah squealed with delight to see them, but Abigail was unimpressed, dropping her packages unceremoniously onto the floor of the porch, into the new dusting of snow.

"It's *kald*," she complained. "Are we going to stand out here staring at candles all *nacht?*"

Joseph ignored his daughter's cruel words, even if they pierced at Ruth's heart. It appeared as though Joseph had grown impervious to Abigail's bitterness over the past few weeks, even if Ruth had not.

"You did a beautiful job, didn't she, Leah?" Joseph cooed, picking up his youngest daughter to touch the draping garlands over the porch's eaves. "Look how hard Ruth has worked."

"Happy *Chrischdaag*!" Matthew boomed from the doorway. "We have a feast inside and *sider* to warm you up."

"It's not *Chrischdaag* yet," Abigail insisted, her voice raising, but again, her father ignored her, reaching down to pick up the discarded packages as he set Leah back on her feet.

"That sounds *wunderbar*, Matthew," he agreed with forced cheer, causing Ruth's heart to drop. She wondered if the entire evening would go this way.

Leah scampered through the open door and begrudgingly, her sister followed as Joseph stood behind, unspeaking, but his eyes saying enough. Ruth bit on her lower lip and stared at him, but he only grinned at her.

"Happy *Chrischdaag*, Ruthie."

"Happy *Chrischdaag*," she replied slowly. She wanted to ask about Abigail but thought better of it. Esther's words echoed in her mind.

We won't let the child ruin our Chrischdaag. We will make the best of it, despite her mood, and maybe that will be enough to coax her out of it.

With enough food, cheer and God's love, anything was possible, after all. It was Christmas.

Inside, the children collected in the living room with Matthew and Joseph as Ruth headed into the kitchen for cider and cookies. The turkey was almost ready and while she would not usually serve sweets beforehand, she remembered how well they had gone with Abigail when she had first brought them to the shop.

Loading up a tray with steaming mugs and overflowing cookies, she re-entered the front of the house, forcing a smile on her face as she laid the dishes down on the coffee table.

Abigail had retreated to a corner of the room as the men discussed their respective businesses. Leah began to tear at the packaging of one of the gifts Ruth and Esther had carefully wrapped.

"I think Leah is eager to open some of her presents already," Ruth interrupted her father and Joseph. Embarrassed, Joseph tried to shoo Leah away. Ruth simply shook her head, catching Abigail's interested gaze from the corner of the living room.

"It can't harm to open up one or two before *nachtesse* is ready, can it?" she said. Joseph shrugged indifferently.

"It's up to you," he agreed, settling back as Leah clapped her hands eagerly.

"That one is for you, Leah, but there's another one for your *schweschder* right beside it." Leah did not wait for Ruth to pick up Abigail's gift as she tore into her own, her eyes widening happily to see the handmade doll inside.

"Here, Abby," Ruth offered, gently handing the package to her. Abigail took it, unable to resist the idea of a present. Abigail perched nervously beside Joseph on the sofa and began to frown and Ruth wished she had reconsidered her seating plan, but it was too late now.

"What do you say, Abby?"

The child grunted and undid the paper, her unhappy look deepening when she saw the contents.

"A *dall*?" she whined, looking at Leah's.

"*Yah*," Ruth said eagerly. "It's exactly like Leah's."

"That's *schtupid*," Abigail snapped, throwing it aside.

"Abby!" Joseph cried, color draining out of his face.

"I'm too big for *dall*," she insisted, folding her arms over her chest in her usual way. "I'm seven, not two, like Leah!"

"I-I know that," Ruth agreed, flustered that Abigail had reacted so angrily toward the toy she had spent so many hours making. "But it's not so much for—"

"It's *schtupid*. I'll use it for the fire!"

Joseph stood up abruptly and Abigail's mouth clamped shut.

"Apologize to Ruthie right now," he whispered, his voice shaking. Abigail continued to remain mute, looking away, and Ruth stood, putting her hand on his arm.

"It's fine, Joe," she whispered softly. "Abby is too *auld* for these little *maedel* things anymore, aren't you, Abby? I-I have to be more careful next time."

Her head whipped around toward Ruth, and her eyes narrowed as if to question the "next time" Ruth spoke of.

"I'm going to check on *nachtesse*," Ruth said, excusing herself, hurrying off toward the kitchen. She prayed that no one would follow her and exhaled when neither of the men came. It was only then that she allowed a tear of frustration to slip down her cheek.

Maybe the best thing to do is stop trying, she decided. *I'm only going to make things worse if I keep pushing.*

On Christmas morning, the Rabers and the Beilers gathered together to head toward the Millers where the bishop was hosting the Christmas services on his own, vast property. It was a tradition he had upheld for the past decade, even though worship alternated throughout the households biweekly. Bishop Miller always insisted on holding both Christmas services and Easter at his property.

No one much minded, even those who lived on the far end of Benny's Creek and were forced to make the journey through snowstorms. It meant that the lottery of them hosting the busiest, messiest service of the year would never befall their families. The travel was a small price to pay for the peace of mind.

Although he would never admit it, Bishop Miller was something of a braggart who enjoyed hosting the community at his large home. Still, he was a kind man whose sermons resonated with most, but today, Ruth found it difficult to listen while she tried to keep an eye on Leah.

"Go get your *schweschder*," she instructed Abigail.

"Aren't you her *mudder* now?" Abigail asked coldly. "You should get her."

"Have some respect for your elders, Abigail Raber!" Liza hissed from her place on Esther's left. "Or I'll have the Bishop speak to you again!"

Abigail balked and slipped off the pew to locate her little sister, but when a few minutes passed and Leah returned, Abigail did not.

"You must sit still during worship," Ruth informed Leah softly. "Where is your *schweschder*?"

"Let us pray," one of the ministers intoned from the front of the congregation, his breath escaping in puffs against the cold, winter air. Ruth bowed her head, but her eyes darted around the female section, searching for movement among the black and white prayer bonnets.

"She'll be along," Liza whispered. "Don't worry about the girl."

Ruth could not help but cast Joseph's mother a sidelong look as she tried to focus her energies on prayer.

How can she not worry about her own kinnskin? I should go looking.

But as she moved to stand, Esther's hand shot out and stopped her.

"*Nee*," her sister whispered firmly. "Don't."

Stunned, Ruth sat again slowly. "Why not?" she breathed.

"She's been doing this a lot, running off and expecting someone to *komme* looking for her."

"Shh!" Liza hissed at them, and the women fell silent. Ruth believed her sister, but it did not make her feel any better. Joseph had not mentioned this before and if that were true, where would they find Abigail when they went looking? Outside? Hiding inside?

It was so cold now and heavy snow was predicted soon...

She could hardly sit still, waiting for the service to be over, her gaze now lingering on Joseph, who sat several rows ahead with Eli, his father and Matthew. They did not seem aware that there was anything amiss, and Ruth was not sure she wanted to be the one to tell him.

Oh pliese, just come back, Abby, she begged silently, but the girl did not return, her stubbornness determined to teach them all a lesson.

When the sermons finally concluded, Ruth was the first one up, rushing toward Joseph, panic in her voice.

"Abby—she's gone! She went after Leah and now she's gone!"

To her surprise, Joseph did not seem perturbed by her admission.

"She'll *komme* back," he grumbled, irritated. "On *Chrischdaag*, no less."

"You ought to lock her out of the *haus* one night," David Raber suggested with as much coldness as his wife. "That will teach her to act like a *fuhl*."

"She's a little *maedel, daed*." Joseph sighed. "But I'm not chasing after her. If she wants to sit in the *schnee* and freeze, let her. She'll *komme* back when she wants to open her presents."

"Open her presents!" Liza was appalled as the families made their way toward the food-laden tables. "I would take every one of her gifts and give it to someone worthy of them. She deserves to see that her actions have consequences."

Every word they spoke drove a blade deeper into Ruth's heart. They were talking about a little child, not a woman who was in control of her emotions.

"I'm going to look for her," Ruth informed them.

"*NEE!*" The response was collective, Joseph's voice the loudest. He exhaled and offered her an exhausted smile. "That's what she wants, Ruth. She expects us to meet her every whim and, frankly, I'm tired of it. Don't go after her. She's not lost or in danger. She'll be back."

Ruth swallowed the stone in her throat. She understood his point, but it did not make her feel any better.

"If she's not back in an hour when we're ready to go, we'll both go searching for her," Joseph added, reading her expression. "But I promise you, she will be cold, hungry, and more miserable than before."

"I hope you're right…?"

Joseph chuckled and chucked her chin gently. "*Es dutt mer leed*, Ruthie. You deserve so much better than what you've gotten from her."

Ruth's heart softened, and she shrugged bashfully. "It's a *gut* thing that you make up for it then, isn't it?" she replied sweetly.

"Do I?"

"I think so," she mumbled, blushing as their eyes locked. "You must be doing something right…or it's a *Chrischdaag* miracle."

Joseph began to laugh heartily and suddenly she realized just how close they stood to the rest of their family. But when she looked to the others, they cast the couple coy, appreciative smiles and Ruth saw that they approved of the match.

Suddenly, Esther called out. "There she is!"

Ruth's euphoria in Joseph's attention was short-lived as the small crowd parted and an infuriated Abigail appeared in front of them.

"Didn't you even notice I was gone?!" she shouted. "I was gone for a whole hour!"

Ruth started to agree that they had noticed, but Joseph interjected.

"We have been too busy celebrating *Chrischdaag* as a *familye*, Abby. Would you like to do that with us?"

Ruth cringed internally as naked animosity illuminated her small face, but Joseph had already turned his back on her, refusing to cater to her uprising temper tantrum.

"I'm *hungerich*," he announced. "Let's *esse*! *Komme*, Ruthie. I think I see your *eepies* in the corner, don't I?"

He steered her away from his sulking daughter, his voice low. "We will enjoy our first *Chrischdaag* together and pray that *Gott hilf* Abby find the peace that she needs."

Ruth cast the girl a glance over her shoulder, but the girl had disappeared again.

This is not the way I had hoped to spend Chrischdaag, she thought mournfully. *But Old Chrischdaag will be better. We'll make sure of it.*

CHAPTER 6

*B*ut with all of Ruth's best intentions, there seemed to be no way of getting closer to Abigail in the days following Christmas.

The child made it a point to hide herself away whenever Ruth visited the Raber household and when Joseph came to the Bielers, he often only had Leah with him.

"She refuses to *komme* here," he admitted when Ruth asked. "If I insist, she starts to fight with me and runs out of the *haus*."

Matthew, who had overheard the conversation, made a reproving sound with his tongue.

"Joey, you can't let her dictate how to run your *haus*."

"You sound like my *mudder*," Joseph countered staunchly, the stress on his face tangible. Ruth glanced at her father and shook her blonde braid imperceivably. It was clear that Joseph did not need more lectures right now, but a solution.

Leah had scampered off somewhere and Ruth instructed her father to find the little girl before the toddler found herself in trouble.

When she and Joseph were alone, she turned to him, her heart beating faster with concern as she closed the distance between them in the kitchen.

"Joey…"

"Don't say it," he insisted, holding up his hand as if he already knew what she was going to suggest. "I've heard enough '*adweis*' on how to handle Abby."

"*Nee*," Ruth countered slowly, reaching gently for his hand. "I wasn't going to give you advice. I was going to suggest that we…"

She inhaled and lowered her eyes. "We stop seeing one another."

Joseph's head jerked up as if he had been struck, panic overtaking his face. "*NEE!*" he cried out without hesitation, his cheeks paling in dismay. "*Nee*, Ruthie, that's…*nee!*"

He shook his head vehemently and sighed deeply, pain creasing his handsome features as he rubbed his beard vigorously. "That's not a solution. As much as my *mudder's* ways upset me, she and my *vadder* are right. You are needed in our lives. Leah adores you."

Joseph stared down at her fingers. "Abby has always been a difficult *kin*. Maybe she was *kippisch* of the attention the new *bobbli* got when Leah arrived, but she changed after. Emma noticed, but she was so *bissi* with the *bobbli* that Abby got more cast aside…"

He faltered again and Ruth exhaled, squeezing his hand softly. "I wish we had paid more mind to her then. Maybe we wouldn't have the problems we have now."

"She simply needs a little extra attention."

"But to give it to her shows her that she's winning with this poor attitude and her demands. I don't know whether I can cope with it."

"Neither can we cope with all this fighting and bickering—especially not during *Chrischdaag*, Joey," Ruth insisted. "And she keeps running off?"

Joseph exhaled again, this time pulling his hands away, and Ruth bit on her lower lip, glancing at the piles of food sitting on the counter. Like the rest of the families in the community, she was getting ready for the joint supper for old Christmas on Sunday after worship. There was much to do, much to prepare for before the massive feast was to take place, but Ruth was more concerned about the pressing issue growing worse, not better as everyone seemed to believe.

"I've spoken to her time and again about that foolishness," Joseph grumbled, sitting on one of the wooden chairs, to bury his face in his hands. "She always comes back, sulking and angrier than ever, but it's getting so *kald*—"

"They're saying there is going to be a storm over the next week, Joe. You can't let her keep doing this."

Ruth immediately bit on her lower lip and apologized, hearing herself lecturing him as so many had already before. "I know you're trying your best and are at your wits' end now. I have also been wracking my brain on how to make things easier, but it feels like the harder I try, the worse it gets."

"She isn't making things easy," Joseph conceded.

He raised his eyes and their stares met silently for a moment.

"I feel as though you're the only one getting me through this *Chrischdaag*," he murmured. "*Pliese*, don't talk about ending things now."

Ruth's heart softened at the sincerity of his words, and she nodded in agreement. "Okay," she conceded. "I won't. We'll try to make it through *auld Chrischdaag* and pray for the best."

"*Gott* will see us through," Joseph insisted, but to Ruth's ears it sounded as if he was trying to convince himself, not her.

"*Yah*, He will," she agreed with more firmness. "He always does, doesn't He?"

○○○

On the Saturday evening before Old Christmas, Joseph brought both girls to the house to help with the final preparations.

Leah instantly ran into Ruth's arms, almost slipping up the snowy steps as flakes fell fast from the darkening sky overhead.

"Careful, *liebling*!" Ruth gasped, catching the little girl before she could fall, her pulse racing as she took in the heavy snowfall encasing the landscape around them. Abigail stomped her boots toward the door, her head held high as Matthew called a greeting, but she ignored all the adults, pushing her way inside. Ruth and Joseph exchanged a look, but he shook his head.

"Nevermind her," Joseph insisted, ushering his daughter and Ruth inside. "There's a storm *cooma*, *yah*? I heard them talking today in the store. They think it will be ten inches *dienacht* and continuing through to the *mariye*, if not the afternoon."

Worry shot through Ruth as she closed the door, taking Joseph's coat and hat to hang on the rack near the staircase.

"Oh, I hope that's not true," she mumbled, again looking toward the windows as if to will away the white. "Not *dienacht*."

She was about to turn and follow the others into the house when the snort of a horse from outside stopped her and she turned fully back toward the door again.

"Are you expecting someone else?" Joseph asked, pausing in the hallway, also catching the noise from the yard.

Ruth shook her head, throwing the door back open.

Henry Fischer and his wife, Sarah, dismounted the bench of their buggy, the pair shivering as they slid up the front of the Bieler house.

"Henry! Sarah!" Ruth called in surprise. "*Wat* are you doing here? *Komme* inside. You'll catch your deaths out here."

They stopped at the foot of the snowy stairs, shaking their heads in unison.

"*Nee*, Ruthie," the minister rasped, his words escaping in plumes of steam against the cold air. "We can't stay. We're going to all the *landsmann*."

Alarm crept down Ruth's spine at the revelation and she hurried forward, forgetting that she had already removed her boots, her socked feet crunching against the ice. Shivering, she stared at them blankly. "*Wei*? What happened?"

Sarah waved behind her vaguely and released a mirthless chuckle. "*Gott*," she replied, looking upwards. "We can't have the service or *nachtesse* like this. The weather is going to be too bad *mariye*. It's too dangerous for traveling."

Dismayed, Ruth gaped at her as Joseph joined her side.

"You're canceling *auld Chrischdaag*?" he echoed.

"Just until the storm passes," Henry reassured him. "You wouldn't want to bring little Leah out in this *kald*. *Wat* if your *waegel* gets stuck? It's not safe. You're best staying *deheem*. We'll reschedule it."

He gestured for his wife to follow him, and the pair turned back toward their waiting buggy as Ruth stared after them in frustration. All of her hard work over the past days had been for nothing, the food in the kitchen bound to spoil by the time the next dinner was scheduled.

"Ruthie, your feet!" Joseph exclaimed, realizing that she wasn't wearing anything but her woolen socks that were becoming damper by the second.

"It's fine," she muttered angrily, moving back toward the house.

As soon as she entered, Abigail's raised voice met her ears.

"*Nee*, I don't want it!" the girl cried at Ruth's father.

"*Wat* is going on in here?" Ruth demanded, turning around the corner to find her father frowning at the girl. Leah began to cry as her father appeared, the toddler pointing at Abigail.

"Abby…" Joseph sighed. "*Wat* is it now?"

"I only offered her some *sider*," Matthew grumbled, sitting on his favorite chair and rolling his eyes skyward.

"And I said I don't want it."

"You may as well drink it," Ruth grouched, making her way toward the kitchen. "It will all go to waste now."

"*Wu* was at the door?" Matthew called after her. Ruth did not respond, her upset stealing her voice for a moment. She busied herself in the kitchen, packing up the dishes she had worked so hard on for the past days, unsure of what she would do with all the food now.

"Ruthie, don't fret about it," Joseph told her calmly, approaching from the hall. "The *schnee* will end, eventually."

"You'll have to bring this *deheem* with you," she told him, swallowing the bitterness in her throat. "Some of it will keep, but I don't have the room—"

Joseph caught her midsentence by wrapping his arm around her waist and turning her toward him. "It's all right, Ruthie," he reassured her tenderly. "It's just a little setback. We'll have *auld Chrischdaag* at our *haus*, *yah*? We can bring all the *esse* to our *haus dienacht* and eat there in the *mariye*. You and Matthew can *komme*. Esther will be happy to see you."

Ruth began to relax at the idea of a small, private family dinner for old Christmas, the disappointment dissipating when Abigail's voice fired out like a shot.

"*NEE!*"

Gasping, she whirled out of Joseph's arms and looked at Abigail's incensed face. "*NEE!* They can't *komme*! They aren't invited!"

"Abby, that's enough!" Joseph snapped. "Go into the other room!"

"*NEE!*" she shouted, hysteria tinging her tone. "I want to go *deheem!*"

"We're not going *deheem*, not yet," Joseph insisted firmly. "You'll go—"

The girl did not allow her father to finish her sentence, spinning around to run through the hallway toward the front door.

"*Wat* is she doing?" Ruth demanded, aghast as a cold blast of wind filled the house. "She's running outside!"

"ABBY!" Joseph choked, taking off after her, Ruth on his heels.

"She's not wearing a coat!" Ruth cried, realizing how ill-equipped the little girl was against the elements. In her anger, she had fled the house without so much as a hat, scarf, or coat.

"She's not wearing boots either!" Matthew called, joining them at the open front door.

The night and snow made visibility terrible now, and Abigail was barely a spec in front of them. "ABBY!" they yelled, their voices carrying off in the wind.

"ABBY *KOMME* BACK!"

It was impossible to tell if she heard or turned to look at them as the couple looked helplessly at one another.

"We have to go after her," Ruth sputtered as Joseph stood, stunned that his eldest daughter would be so reckless. "She'll die out there!"

"*Yah*, you have to go," Matthew conceded. "I'll stay here with the little one. Go now before you lose sight of her."

Without waiting for Joseph to regain his composure, Abigail threw on the closest outer clothing she could find, her boots barely on her feet as she raced into the whistling wind, again calling out for Abigail.

"ABBY?" she yelled. "ABBY WHERE DID YOU GO?"

Through her limited peripheral vision, she saw Joseph struggling against the worsening storm as he made his way down the stairs and toward her, his eyes trained on the ground for Abigail's footprints.

Ruth began to silently pray as tears froze in her eyes.

Pliese, Gott, she knows not what she does. She's just a scared little maedel. Keep her safe.

CHAPTER 7

We should have brought a lamp. Why didn't we bring a lamp?

Joseph's head swam, his cheeks burning with cold against the frosty bites of snow and wind. The storm had grown much worse since he had arrived at the Bieler's with his daughters and he could not see anything but the blinding white in front of his face, the hem of Ruth's cornflower blue dress guiding him.

Every step they took caked her more in precipitation, but that did not slow her down, her trudging steps determined as she continued to call out every two feet.

"*Pliese*, Abby, we're not angry. *Pliese, komme* out! Show us where you are," she begged.

"Abby!" he called, his voice cracking, a dozen horrific images popping into his mind, one after the other, as he struggled through.

I'm sorry, Emma. I tried to keep them safe, he told his lost wife. *She was never happy.*

"ABBY!" Ruth's voice brought him back to the bitter cold, his face frozen now as they headed deeper into the fields. The neighbor's house appeared in the distance, the hazy flicker of their lights a small beacon of hope in their mounting bleakness.

"Could she have gone to the Yoders?" Joseph asked, but Ruth was already heading purposefully toward the house as he hurried to keep up with her.

"Search around the creek," she called back to him. "I'll go speak with them."

"Stay with them," Joseph begged her. "It's only getting worse out here, Ruthie."

She stopped in her tracks and stared at him, snowflakes catching over her lashes, her eyes wide and solemn.

"I won't stop searching until we've found our *maedel*," she told him earnestly, and Joseph wanted to sob. After all the misery Abigail had instilled upon Ruth, she was still willing to lay down her life.

"We'll find her, Joey," Ruth promised him, cupping his face. It was only then that he recognized that she was not wearing mittens.

"Oh, Ruthie…"

"Go now," she insisted, stepping back. "You're right. The weather is getting worse with every passing minute. If we don't find her soon, we'll be trapped out here."

She did not say what she was undoubtedly thinking—that without shoes or a coat, Abigail did not stand a chance against these elements.

Ruth hurried off into the darkness, but on a whim, he followed after her, suddenly afraid to be separated from her. He had seen blizzards like this one before. It would not take much for the snow to hide and part them, even in the daylight. At this time of night, without a moon to guide them, they were blind.

"Goodness!" Michael Yoder declared when he opened the door to the shivering pair on his porch. "*Komme* inside!"

"*Nee!*" the couple answered in unison.

"H-have you seen Abby?" Ruth said, shuddering, rubbing her hands against her arms. Joseph moved closer to her, not caring that the neighbor stared at them strangely.

"Your *maedel*?" Michael asked in confusion, his wife appearing.

"*Komme* inside and close the door, Mike!" she ordered her husband. "You're letting out all the heat!"

"She hasn't been here," Ruth said, turning away.

"Why would a *maedel* that small be out at this hour? In this weather?" Michael called out to them, but Joseph ignored his questions, hurrying after Ruth, who trudged back along the thickening snow, shaking the flakes off her head.

Panting now, they found themselves back in the darkness and Joseph was discombobulated until he felt Ruth's hand in his. It was shockingly warm, despite her earlier tremors.

"It's all right, Joey," she murmured. "Take a breath."

It was only then that he realized his breathing was erratic, and he was shaking violently.

"The creek is this way," she told him, nodding over his shoulder. "Would she have gone there?"

"She has nothing on," he moaned, every minute wasting, twisting his heart as the outcome seemed more dire. "She's freezing."

"And we'll find her," Ruth said again patiently. "Let's go toward the creek anyway and then head back toward the *haus*. Maybe she has returned by now."

Joseph nodded, swallowing the stone in his throat. She always came back. Maybe she had been hiding close by all along, waiting to see if they would go after her. That was all she wanted after all, to be seen.

"All right," he managed to agree, following her lead. But every step became harder as the wind grew gustier, knocking the breath out of him. Several times, they stumbled and were forced to stop as they fell. Joseph clung to Ruth.

Which is worse? Going up the hill or down?

"What is that?!" Joseph straightened his shoulders suddenly, pointing to his right. Ruth followed his finger and saw the small shed, still part of the Yoder property, near the creek.

"I don't know it," she admitted, straining her sopping head forward to see. Caked in ice now, she seemed part snowman as she looked, her eyes popping slightly. "There's a light on in there, Joey!"

Moving as fast as they could in the slippery conditions, the pair made it to the door of the shed, pulling open the half-secured door, already piled up with snow.

"ABBY?" Joseph coughed out, a fit overtaking him as he stumbled into the outbuilding. His eyes adjusted to the dim light casted off by the kerosene lamp in the corner…and then the small, shivering figure, huddled in the corner. "ABBY!"

He rushed toward her as Ruth hurried in behind him. "Is she all right? Is she…?"

Ruth did not finish her sentence, but an exhale filled his ears as he scooped his daughter into his arms and Abigail burst into tears.

"*Es dutt mer leed!*" she sobbed, the tears freezing on her pale face. Her lips had taken on a bluish tinge, and fear clutched Joseph's heart at the sight of his half-frozen daughter.

"It's all right, *liebling*," he told her gruffly, a fusion of anger and relief overwhelming him. "*Komme*. We'll get you *deheem, yah?*"

Ruth's coat fell over them as he rose to carry his daughter out of the shed.

"*Nee*, Ruthie! You need it!" he insisted, but Ruth shook her head.

"It's not far, and she has *nix*. She needs it more than I do. Don't argue with me about it, Joey. Let's get back to the *haus*. We have a lamp now. It will be easier."

She showed the kerosene lamp in her hand that she had picked up from the corner of the tiny shed and nodded toward the door. "*Komme* now."

"*Es dutt mer leed,*" Abigail moaned again.

"Shh, Abby," Joseph urged her, worried about her pallor and the way she repeated herself. "Everything will be okay."

"I'm *mied*," Abby mumbled. "*Daed*, can I go to sleep?"

Joseph did not respond to his daughter and instead turned his attention back to Ruth. "Let's go," he whispered, and she wasted no more time lingering in the musty smelling shack. She reached for the door and pushed, but nothing happened.

Again, she pushed and dread rushed through Joseph.

"Here," he mumbled, extending Abigail toward her. "Take Abby."

Ruth held out her arms, a frown forming on her face in the shadowy light. "Are you hurt, *liebling*?" she asked Abby, but the child appeared to be drifting off to sleep.

"Abby!" Ruth said sharply. "Abby, look at me!"

The girl mumbled something incoherently as Joseph pushed his weight against the door, but like Ruth, he had little luck in moving it. He stared at her in dismay. "We were barely in here a minute!"

"The *schnee* came in too fast," Ruth muttered, her concerned eyes fixed on Abby's drowsy face. "ABBY!"

Abby's eyes flickered back open.

"You have to stay awake, *yah*?"

"Why?" she moaned. "I'm *mied*."

"I know you are tired," Ruth told her as Joseph threw his entire body weight again against the door. Ruth seemed to see that it wasn't budging and moved back toward the ground, looking for something to place between Abigail and the cold. "But if you sleep, it's dangerous, *yah*? *Pliese*, stay awake, Abby. It's important, okay?"

His shoulder now throbbing, a new kind of dread formed in the pit of Joseph's gut as he understood Ruth's unspoken words.

He stumbled toward his daughter, reaching for her, and Ruth handed her back to him as he pressed her urgently to his chest, eager to warm her frozen body against his.

"You stay awake, *yah?*" he told his child tersely. "Whatever you do, Abby, you don't close your eyes."

"Why, *Daed?*" Her words slurred, sending more rounds of terror through Joseph's soul.

"Because we need you to stay awake and tell us stories," Ruth explained quietly. "Can you tell us stories, Abby? Your *vadder* and I have been walking a long time and can't think of any now."

Limply, Ruth turned her head to look dully at Ruth. "Stories?" she echoed.

"*Yah*. Do you know any *gut* stories? We're going to be here for a little bit it seems and while we don't have any *eepies* or *sider*, we still have each other, don't we?"

How she managed to smile through all this, Joseph would never understand, but he was sure he had never loved another as much as he did Ruth in that moment. Abigail looked at her face through hazy, foggy eyes.

"I-I know a story," she agreed. "I-I heard it at *schul.*"

"Oh, I want to hear it, *pliese*," Ruth told her eagerly, settling on the frozen ground. She looked at Joseph, and he held his daughter tighter, also sitting.

Blinking away tears of sorrow, the fear that he might lose his daughter so soon after he had lost his wife attacked Joseph with such ferocity, he could hardly stand it.

In a wavering voice, Abigail began to tell a tale about a rabbit who had lost its way in the forest as the wind outside whipped furiously against the wooden shed, causing Ruth to close her eyes with every blow against the windows.

All Joseph could do was pray and do his best to hold it all together for the sake of his daughter—and the woman he now realized he loved.

CHAPTER 8

Ruth had never been so cold, but she refused to let Joseph or Abigail see it, the child's health far more concerning than her own in that moment. She was certain that they had found Abigail at the bad end of hypothermia. It had been many years since Ruth had seen anyone in this state. Not since David Hertz had been brought back to safety, where he could be warmed by the fire.

Here, in a six-by-six shack with nothing but a quickly burning kerosene lamp for heat and light, and wind seeping through the cracks, Abigail's changes increasing with each passing second but for the heat of her father's body.

"...asked the turtle, 'can you help me find my way *deheem?*'" Abigail mumbled, her words cutting in and out, her voice growing sluggish.

"And what did the turtle say?" Ruth pressed, eying Joseph with concern. She could not be sure if he understood the severity of the situation, but she did not want to speak the words aloud, lest they scare the girl more.

"Hmm?"

"Abby!" Joseph urged sharply, shaking the child in his arms. "You must keep your eyes open."

Ruth heard the anxiety in his tone.

"Can we go *deheem*?" Abigail mumbled. "I want to go *deheem*? I don't like it here, *Daed*."

"We'll go home soon," Joseph promised her, emotion thickening his words.

"I want to go *deheem* now..."

"We can't, not yet," Ruth interjected primly, worried that Joseph might break down if he continued to speak. "There's too much snow to walk outside right now, but when it stops, we'll be on our way, *yah*? Can't you tell me what happened with the rabbit? I want to know."

Tears filled Abigail's luminous eyes in the shadowy shed, her tangled, wet hair sticking to the side of her pale face. "Is this because I ran away?" she rasped, a sob in her throat. "*Es dutt mer leed.* I-I won't do that anymore! *Pliese,* let me *komme deheem*!"

Ruth slid closer, extending a hand toward her, but she was wary to touch the usually defiant child, knowing how easily Abigail snarled. "*Nee*, Abby," she promised. "Of course it's not because you ran off. We came looking for you, didn't we?"

Tears began to slide down her cheeks, and she buried her face in her father's chest. "I didn't think you would *komme*. You never *komme* when I run off."

Ruth's chest tightened as Joseph spoke, his arms tightening protectively around her. "That's no way to get my attention, Abigail," he told her, his words squeaking. "That's not the right way to do things. You're smart enough to know that by now."

"*Yah*, I know," Abigail sniffed. "But that's why I thought you wouldn't *komme* now. I thought you would leave me here all *nacht*."

"Oh, Abby, we would never..." Joseph choked, hugging her tightly. Together, father and daughter cried as Ruth dabbed at her own frigid face, subtly blowing hot air into her hands. But she was not as covert as she had thought, and Joseph saw her.

"*Komme* here, Ruthie," he instructed her, extending his arms. As if on cue to his words, a blast of powerful wind pounded at the shed, forcing a yelp from both the females, and Ruth did not argue, slipping even closer to the pair.

She did not care about modesty or appropriateness, not when their lives were on the line in that moment. Without a coat of her own or heat, their odds of surviving the storm diminished with every minute that passed.

"I don't want to hear a peep out of you, Abigail," Joseph told his daughter warningly, but she said nothing, allowing Ruth to enter the fold of her father's arms. Ruth welcomed the small bounty of heat that he provided, but after a moment, the child again burst into tears.

"We're going to die out here, aren't we?" she wailed.

"*NEE!*" the adults chorused bluntly.

"*Nee*, of course not," Ruth insisted, although she was not sure she should lie to the child. She had no idea what God had planned for them that glacial, unforgiving night. "The storm will pass as storms do and then we can go."

Unexpectedly, Abigail sat up, shaking her head. "But how?" she insisted. "We can't get out!"

Goosebumps prickled at Ruth's arms, raising every blonde hair, but she refused to let Abigail see.

"My *vadder* will *komme* looking for us," Ruth offered confidently. The answer appeared to placate Abigail for a moment, but Ruth caught the uncertainty in Joseph's eye. She had no doubt that her father would come searching for her, but he had no idea where to look. There had been talk of the storm going into the next afternoon and if that happened…

She shuddered again.

"Will he know where to find us?" Abigail asked. Ruth swallowed a groan. She did not want to lie to the child, but it was the only option to stop her from panicking.

"*Gott* will see us through this, Abby," Ruth told her earnestly. "He always has a plan, and we must always trust in it, *yah*?"

"He took my *mudder* from me," Abigail replied sullenly, turning her head away. "I don't trust in anything He does."

"Abby…" Joseph sighed.

"It's all right, Joe," Ruth murmured, reaching for the little girl again. "Did you know that my *mudder* died too when I was *yung* like you?"

Tentatively, Abigail darted her gaze back toward Ruth. "*Yah*?"

"I was very angry with *Gott* for a long time…" Another shiver seized Ruth, and Joseph held her closer. It subsided and Ruth exhaled.

"You're not mad at Him anymore for taking her?" Abigail demanded. "Why not? Didn't you *lieb* your *mudder*?"

"I loved her so very much—as much as you love yours," Ruth replied honestly. "But *my vadder* told me what I'm telling you now, that *Gott* needed her more than we do and that we were left here for special reasons."

Confused, Abigail gawked at her. "What reasons?"

"In my case," Ruth mumbled, trying desperately to keep her teeth from chattering. "It was to take care of my little *schweschder*—Esther."

She offered Abigail a small smile. "Don't you have a little *schweschder* too?"

Understanding illuminated Abigail's face as Joseph closed his eyes. Ruth wondered if he was blinking back tears, but she did not ask.

"*Gott* left me here to take care of Leah?" she whispered. Ruth shrugged and shifted closer, trying to suck what semblance of heat she could through the thin material of her dress. To her relief, she felt most of the warmth radiating off Abigail.

She's warming up! She's more coherent. She might overcome this... if we get out of here on time.

But they did not have water or food...

Ruth did not let her mind venture onto the dark side.

"Leah is waiting for you," Ruth intoned, silently willing the girl to hang on and live. Joseph found her hand and held it tightly and again, Ruth felt tears well in her eyes.

Nee, nee, I can't cry. I can't let Abby see me cry.

"*Gott* is *gut*," Abigail decided, smiling for the first time. "He wants me to take care of Leah."

"That's right," Joseph murmured. "He is *gut*."

Outside, the wind whistled louder, and the snow piled higher against the shed, burying them deeper inside, but the snow walls seemed to insulate the trio from the wind a bit better.

"Will you tell us how the story ends, Abby?" Ruth asked after a small silence. "I'd like to know if the rabbit found his way *deheem*."

But when she looked, the child had fallen asleep against her father's chest. Hesitantly, Ruth looked at Joseph, unsure if he should wake her.

"I don't think she's hypothermic anymore," Joseph whispered, his voice so quiet Ruth had to strain against the howling wind to hear. "But even if she is, we can't keep her up all night. We won't be able to."

Ruth nodded, biting on her lower lip as she glanced at the lamp, wondering how much longer they had until it ran out of fuel.

"Does it make any sense to bang on the door? In case someone came looking for us?" Joseph suggested, but Ruth shook her head.

"No one would be foolish enough. My *vadder* has Leah, remember, and no one else knows we're out here. No one would *komme* until after the storm. We would only be wasting our breaths and energy—and waking up and scaring Abby."

She settled back against the man and his daughter, gently pulling her hand out of Joseph's to slide Abigail's tangled dark strands away from her face.

"You are *wunderbar* with her," Joseph told her sweetly. "I wish she hadn't spent so much time fighting with you."

Ruth smiled, continuing to stroke Abigail's hair gently. "She's not so bad when she's not screaming," she agreed, and Joseph chuckled.

"*Nee*. She's not."

"Do you think this will change anything between us?" Ruth asked. She was immediately embarrassed. She had not meant to ask the question aloud.

"If we make it through, I hope so."

Ruth jerked her head up and narrowed her eyes. "Don't say that," she chided him fiercely. "The storm will pass. They all do."

Joseph's mouth parted, but that was the last thing that Ruth saw before they were plunged into complete blackness.

Her heart leapt into her throat and she swallowed it back.

"There's no more kerosene," she rasped nervously.

"*Nee*," Joseph agreed tersely. For a moment, she did nothing but remain in place, but when she started to move, Joseph pulled her back.

"*Nee*, don't," he told her. "Stay where you are."

"Why?"

"Because it's safest if we all stay together now until the sun comes up."

His strong arm wrapped around her shoulder and he pulled her back, sandwiching Abigail between them to ensure she was the warmest. And then there was nothing but silence except for the eerie shriek of the winter wind outside, threatening to take them all in the night.

CHAPTER 9

*L*oud coughing awoke Ruth from a fitful sleep, one she had not realized she had fallen into in the first place. Her limbs were numb, fingers and toes frozen and difficult to move as she struggled to wiggle them in the cold, gray light filtering through the shed.

It took her several seconds to realize it was Joseph who was coughing, and she raised her stiff body out of his solid hold, his arms apparently never releasing either her or Abigail throughout the night that they had somehow managed to make it through. Instinctively, she turned to look for the child who remained asleep, her small chest rising and falling evenly, much to Ruth's relief. Only then did she meet Joseph's eyes, his coughing dying away as he eyed her apologetically.

"I woke you," he mumbled in a low tone.

"It wasn't much of a sleep," she admitted, smiling weakly as she untangled herself from his hold to rise from the floor. Every movement was agony, her bones creaking from the cold she had endured overnight, pains affecting her in regions she had not known she had.

"Is the storm done?" Joseph whispered, hugging his daughter closer. Ruth had no answer for him yet as she strained to look out of the high windows, but the grayish light gave her some hope. It seemed too bright for snow, and the brash wind that had assaulted the small shed the previous night had died out completely.

"I think so..." she finally offered, turning back to look at him. Relief overtook Joseph's face, and Abigail stirred awake with a long moan.

"D-daed...?"

"I'm here, *liebling*," he reassured her quickly. "It's all right."

Abigail's eyes fluttered open, and she stared at Ruth in front of her, blinking wildly. "Is it *mariye*?"

"*Yah*," Ruth told her, rejoining them. "Soon, *hilf* will be here."

"How?" Abigail asked sullenly and Ruth's heart sank. It seemed the morning light had brought back the same girl she had always been.

"We didn't return last *nacht*," Joseph reminded her patiently. "Matthew will be wondering where we are."

Ruth did not say what she was thinking aloud. With Leah to care for and the snow undoubtedly piled high enough to block in the most seasoned of farmer, how could they expect her father to come looking immediately?

"We need to pray now, Abby," Ruth told her urgently, her stomach rumbling. The noise seemed to reverberate off the walls of the tiny building, reminding all of them that they had no resources and were running out of time.

Father and daughter perched into sitting positions, and Ruth reached for their hands, bowing her head. "Today is *auld Chrischdaag*," she told them. "*Gott* would not forsake us today, of all days."

Abigail made a whimpering noise, but she did not argue Ruth's point as she, too, hung her head. Whether she was too weak or simply too defeated, Ruth could not say, but she was glad for the few minutes of silence as they all prayed vehemently to God for salvation.

It was all they could do. Pray and wait. And hope.

Time was difficult to gauge, but the snow and wind did not return, and hints of sunny rays struggled through the sooty clouds, casting something of a glow inside the shed.

"Is it still *mariye*?" Abigail asked sleepily sometime later. Ruth had no answer for her. It was hard to know.

"Why don't you rest, liebling?" Joseph suggested.

"No one is *cooma* for us," Abigail said. There was no anguish in her voice now, only certainty. "We're going to die here."

To hear such morbid talk from the mouth of a child so young was enough to motivate her father to his feet and move toward the door. With a grunt, he tried with all his might to push against it, despite Ruth's pleadings.

"You need to save your strength, Joey," she told him firmly. "There's too much *schnee*. It wouldn't have melted yet."

"The sun has been out for some time now," he insisted stubbornly.

"Even so, the temperatures are below freezing!" she replied. "*Pliese*, Joseph—"

Abruptly, he held up his hand. "SHH!"

With his head cocked and his pupils dilated, he waved her closer. "Listen!"

Ruth's heart leapt, and she hurried toward the door where Joseph had pressed his ear. "What is it?"

Her gaze darted back toward Abigail, who had followed her father's advice and returned to sleep on the hard, uncomfortable ground. Again, Joseph waved at her to be silent and Ruth worried that he might be getting cabin fever.

"Joey—"

"SHH!" he insisted. "Listen! There's something out there!"

Warily, Ruth eyed him but did as he instructed, pushing her own ear against the wood. She waited, biting on her lower lip.

What will I do if he starts to unravel in here? I can't handle a sickly maedel and a narricht mann.

The notion filled her with panic. But as she lifted her head, she suddenly heard what Joseph had heard. Distinctly and in the distance, a gentle crunching.

Her eyes popped. "Something is out there!" she squeaked, falling back.

"I told you!" He laughed, relieved that she had heard it too.

"It could be an animal. A deer or fox."

"It could be," he agreed, and her shoulders sagged with relief as she realized he was not losing his mind. "But we should make noise just in case it's someone looking for us."

In unison, they began to pound on the door of the cabin, Ruth praying simultaneously.

"*HALLO!*" Joseph yelled. "*HALLO,* CAN YOU HEAR US?"

His noises woke Abigail, who whimpered. "What's going on?"

Neither of the adults responded at first, not wanting to miss the opportunity of being rescued if the moment presented itself, but when tears began to fall down her cheeks, Ruth rushed to her side.

"Don't be afraid, Abby," she begged the girl. "Someone might be out there. We're trying to get their attention."

She took Abigail's hand and smiled reassuringly. "We want to go *deheem, yah?*"

Hope colored Abigail's tear-stained cheeks as she nodded, but before she could speak, a faraway voice responded to Joseph's call.

"JOEY?!"

Joseph's knees buckled and Ruth leapt to her feet, running back toward the door.

"ELI!" she screamed, banging harder against the door where Joseph had left off. "ELI! *HILF* US!"

The crackling of snow under foot got closer and Ruth realized that it was more than one set of footsteps.

"Ruthie?" Eli was outside the door now, his voice heavy with happiness. "Esther has been out of her mind with worry. Is Abby with you?"

"*Yah*, she's here," Ruth told him. "Everyone is ok for now, but we have no heat, water, or *esse*. We've been here for hours and are sharing two coats between the three of us. Abby has no shoes. I suspect she's mildly hypothermic, but we're doing our best to keep her warm with body heat. The situation is not *gut*. You must get us out of here."

Joseph returned to his daughter, the reminder of her poor condition inspiring him to wrap her back up in his arms.

"We'll get you out," Eli told Ruth calmly. "It will take some time, though. The *schnee*…"

"*Pliese* hurry, Eli…"

Scraping interrupted her plea, Eli already getting to work as Ruth retreated to Joseph and Abigail, gnawing on the insides of her cheeks in anticipation. The sound of another shovel joining the dig gave her faith that they would be freed sooner than she had anticipated, but it seemed to be taking forever.

"*Wat* if they can't get us out?" Abigail moaned, her teeth chattering again. "What if we're trapped here?"

Her irrational fears were fueled by hunger and tiredness.

"We're almost out, *liebling*," Ruth told her reasonably. "We just need to be patient now."

Joseph placed both his arms around them, drawing them against his chest and Abigail was once more pressed between them as she had been in the night, calmed by the rhythm of their joint heartbeats as the scraping and cracking of ice and snow outside got closer and louder.

Abruptly, the door opened and a blast of icy wind overtook Ruth, knocking the breath out of her.

Eli, Michael Yoder, and David Raber stood at the threshold, blinking in disbelief at the sight in front of them. Eli grinned as his father and the owner of the shed frowned reprovingly.

"Where is your coat, Ruth?" David demanded. Painfully, Ruth struggled to stand as Abigail explained.

"She gave it to me."

David's frown deepened. "And why didn't you have a coat? And what were you even doing out? You caused so much trouble, Abigail!"

"That's enough, *Daed*," Joseph retorted, standing and picking up his daughter in his arms, wrapping his jacket around her. He handed Ruth's coat back to her, and she put it back on, relishing the smell of Joseph on it.

"What happened here last *nacht*?" Michael Yoder demanded. "In my shed, no less?"

He shook his head.

"I would hope that you would rather find us alive in your shed than dead in your field," Ruth said sharply, trudging out into the deep snow after Eli. The younger man chuckled, but Michael was not amused.

"You could have just *komme* to the *haus*," he insisted.

"It was so much more comfortable here," Joseph quipped. "Like Joseph found the barn in the Bible. If only you'd supplied us with a manger, Mike."

Michael grumbled and stomped awkwardly through the thick snow toward his house as Ruth cast Joseph a wry grin. Their gazes lingered a moment before they hurried off toward Eli's waiting wagon.

"It's going to be an uncomfortable ride back *deheem*," he warned. "But our *haus* is closer."

"My *vadder* will be worried," Ruth told him. "I need to go *deheem*."

"I need to see Leah," Abigail said, speaking for the first time since their rescue. Eli cast them both a wary look.

"And I have so much *esse*," Ruth added sweetly. "You could *komme*…"

Eli laughed weakly. "Oh, all right. Esther will go anywhere you are right now," he agreed. "My *leit* may be harder to convince…"

David Raber appeared at the buggy, shooting his eldest son another disdainful look, but before he could speak, Ruth leaned forward.

"It's *Chrischdaag*, David. Your *kinner* are with you and you have your *weib* and *kinnskinner*. That is more than most can say. You almost lost two of them last *nacht*. Be thankful to *Gott* for what he has given you."

David's face softened slightly.

"*Komme* to our *haus* and *esse*. Celebrate Christ's birth and admire this force of nature from inside where it's warm and Abby can be checked. *Pliese*."

He considered her words carefully and nodded.

"*Yah*, okay," he agreed stiffly. "Because it's *Chrischdaag*."

Ruth settled back and exhaled. To her surprise, Abigail slipped out of her father's hold and snuggled against her side.

"Ruthie…" she whispered.

Ruth stared down at the red-rimmed green eyes. "*Yah, liebling?*"

"Denki."

Surprised, Ruth looked up at Joseph, convinced that he had told her to say something, but he seemed as baffled by her gratitude as she was.

"For what?"

"For...for not leaving."

Tears filled Ruth's eyes, and she gulped back the stone of emotion in her throat.

"I will stay as long as you need me, Abby. That has always been the reason I came around in the first place," she told the girl in a low voice. The buggy began to move tediously across the icy terrain, and Ruth adjusted the blanket carefully around Abigail's neck and shoulders.

The child yawned and dropped her head against Ruth's shoulder.

"And you love my *daed*, too," she mumbled, closing her eyes. Ruth blushed furiously, her chin raising to meet Joseph's eyes. He had heard his daughter's declaration. A slow smile spread over his face and he nodded, his fingers reaching for hers over the thick, wool blanket which covered Abigail's small frame.

Ruth's pulse raced as she accepted his hand, exhaling the stress of the past weeks. Winter wind rushed over her face, the beauty of the snow-capped pines filling her heart with love for the first time all season.

This was what Christmas was meant to be: family, God's divine intervention, and the outpouring of love everywhere. Ruth had never felt it more strongly.

EPILOGUE

ONE YEAR LATER

The sun shone brightly overhead, a hawk swooping down to eye the tables below with far too much interest.

"Get the little dogs in the *haus*," Sarah Fischer ordered to no one in particular, noticing the watchful bird. "Or they'll end up someone's supper."

"Isn't that a cheery thought to have on *auld Chrischdaag*?" Joseph chuckled in Ruth's ear as she set her chicken noodle casserole on the table with the other dishes. Ruth chuckled, her head turning upward to take in the startling blue sky, accented with fluffy white clouds.

"She's vying for position as a Bishop's wife," Ruth reminded her husband.

"She's not doing Henry any favors by bossing everyone around," Joseph insisted.

Ruth shrugged. "I'm content just bossing you around," she teased.

"And me!" Abigail interjected, skipping between them. She batted her pretty, green eyes toward her step-mother and father coyly before dancing away and Ruth rolled her eyes.

"Where's Leah now?" Joseph asked worriedly. "Abby was supposed to be watching her."

"She's with Esther," Ruth told him, nodding toward her own sister. Joseph's younger daughter and Esther chased one another around a tree, Ruth's sister's condition impossible to hide at this point.

"Go find Eli. We should sit down and *esse* soon," Ruth told her husband. "And collect that wayward daughter of yours. I want to speak with Essie a minute."

"No *warrick* today," Joseph scolded lightly. "It's *Chrischdaag*."

Ruth laughed. "*Bobbli* don't wait to be born."

Joseph appeared aghast at the idea of Esther giving birth at the Old Christmas feast. "You don't think--?"

"*Nee*, I don't," she said and laughed. "But I want to talk to my *schweschder* for a minute. Do you mind?"

Joseph shook his head. "Of course not. I'll collect the girls and your *vadder*—wherever he's run off to now. He's as bad as Leah these days."

Chuckling, Joseph wandered away, leaving Ruth to head toward Esther, who had finally stopped with her chase of three-year-old Leah and leaned forward to catch her breath, hands on her knees, her swollen belly protruding outward awkwardly.

"You shouldn't be running around like a teenager," Ruth chided her lightly and Esther laughed.

"I should stay in good form for when the *bobbli komme*," Esther replied nonchalantly, watching Leah affectionately scamper off toward Eli, now that their game was done. Her eyes shone to see her husband with his niece, her thoughts tangible even before she spoke them. "He'll make a *gut vadder*."

"And you'll make a *gut mudder*, too," Ruth replied lightly. Esther flipped her gaze back toward her sister, her smile never faltering.

"I will," she agreed softly. "I learned from the very best after all."

Ruth's heart twisted with pride at the compliment, the heat from a blush staining her cheeks.

"Oh...I don't know about all that," she mumbled, looking away.

"Are you kidding, Ruthie?" Esther stood up to her full height, her hands subconsciously moving toward her belly as her eyes trailed toward the blue sky, a smile quirking her lips against the sunshine. "You were so *yung* when *Mamm* passed, but you stepped in and filled her role with me so easily. I'm not surprised in the least that you won over Abby as quickly as you did."

Ruth laughed aloud.

"Was it quick? It felt like ages to me!"

Esther's smile widened. "It wasn't so long," she replied. "You were able to show her how caring and loving you are, despite how awful she was behaving. If that had been me, I would have given up well before the *nacht* of the storm."

Once again, Ruth found herself looking back toward the heavens, marveling at how much difference a year could make. It hardly felt like winter at all, the cold bearable with the old Christmas feast outdoors for the first time in years.

A light dusting of snow graced Bishop Miller's acres of land and the children had found enough flakes to make snowmen and create snow angels, but after the blizzard that they had endured the year before, Ruth almost considered the light frosting balmy by comparison.

"If not for that storm, she might never have allowed me into her life," Ruth mused, although not for the first time. She had thought many times about the events that had led to her marriage to Joseph over the past year. "And she still gives me problems on occasion."

"That has always been her personality." Esther sighed. "I hope she'll grow out of it one day."

"I'm sure she will," Ruth murmured, casting a look toward her stepchildren who had now located their father. Like Ruth had in the aftermath of her mother's passing, Abigail had learned to accept her role as a leader for her own smaller sibling. Leah did not realize it yet, but one day, she would be having a conversation exactly like this with Abigail.

"*Komme*, let's *esse*," Esther urged. "I'm *hungerich*."

"Wait!"

Stunned by the urgency in her sister's tone, Esther stopped, concern darkening her pretty face. "*Wat* is it, Ruthie?"

Embarrassed, Ruth turned her back to the throng of parishioners, suddenly wishing she had not chosen that minute to pull Esther aside.

"*Nix, nix,*" she mumbled, shaking her head. A wind whipped up, pulling a strand of blonde hair loose from beneath her bonnet, and Ruth hurried to tuck it back nervously.

"Don't say it's nothing. I can read it on your face," Esther insisted, reaching for her arm. She guided Ruth toward the barn and away from any potentially prying ears. "Is something wrong? Is it Joey?"

"*Nee! Nee,* not at all. He's…*wunderbar.*"

A dreamy smile touched her lips as she thought of him and all they had shared in the past months, their lives together, exactly what she had hoped for in a marriage.

"Was I wrong about Abby? Is she still being a *gruuft?*"

Ruth's hands moved idly toward the garland twined through the stalls, pausing over a clump of real gooseberries as she struggled to find the words. They seemed so strange in her mind, on her lips. She could not imagine to say them aloud.

"Ruthie, you're worrying me now," Esther told her urgently and Ruth realized that she had no choice but to say what she had to say or risk upsetting her sister.

"We will have *kossins* to play with one another," she blurted out in a hushed whisper, her face aflame.

At first, Esther merely stared at her, her eyebrows raised as she waited for Ruth to say more, but slowly, understanding overtook her expression.

"You're *ime familye weg!*" she shrieked far too loudly. Ruth pressed her finger to her lips and whipped her chin over her shoulder, certain that someone must have heard her sister's proclamation.

"SHH!" she begged Esther, who had the good sense to offer contrition.

"*Es dutt mer leed!*" She giggled, throwing her arms around her sister. "I-I wasn't expecting that news! You were acting so mysterious. I thought something was wrong."

"I'm sorry," Ruth sighed. "I-I haven't told anyone else yet."

Esther's smile faded. "Not even Joey?"

Ruth shook her head and looked at the straw-laden ground, shifting her toe against the hay.

"Why not?" Esther demanded. "He'll be over the moon!"

"I don't know if he will," Ruth confessed and Esther stepped back to stare at her, dumbfounded.

"Of course he will! *Wat* a thing to say!"

"I mean…*yah*, he will…but things are going so well right now." An unexpected shiver rushed through Ruth and she rubbed her hands over her arms, the memory of last year resurfacing in a torrent. "*Wat* if a *bobbli* only upsets the balance that I've finally found with the girls?"

Esther tutted her tongue and raised a hand to wag a finger scoldingly. "*Nee*! *Nee*, you're not doing that again. You already spent far too much time catering to Abby's wants. This is about you and Joey now, not Abby."

She moved toward the door and Ruth gawked after her. "Where are you going?"

"You stay right here," her sister ordered her. "Don't you move, you hear me?"

She was gone before Ruth could argue and the older woman began to pace around the open space, her heart racing in her ears with such ferocity, she did not notice that Joseph had joined her until he was almost beside her.

"Oh!" she gasped, a hand on her chest. "You startled me."

"Esther told me you were looking for me," he said, appearing baffled by her reaction.

"I'm not—I mean…I am." She inhaled deeply and composed herself, reminding herself that this was her husband now.

Esther is right. This is our life now, our future. Abby should be happy for us. I should have come to Joey first.

"*Liebling*, what is it?" Joseph asked tenderly, reading her distracted expression. "Has Abby done something?"

Ruth chuckled and shook her head. "*Nee*…not yet."

Joseph's frown intensified. "What do you anticipate she's going to do?" he asked warily. "And why?"

"I'm *ime familye weg*," she told him, refusing to drag out the suspense a moment longer. "And I don't think she'll take the news well."

Joseph's entire body collapsed in joy, his strong arms encircling her without a second thought.

"Oh, Ruthie! I-I'm so happy!" he whispered, kissing the top of her head. He laughed heartily and kissed her again. "But you're wrong about Abby."

Ruth drew back to look at him. "How do you know?" she asked, unconvinced.

He smiled happily. "Because only yesterday, she was asking me when she might have a little *bruder* on the way."

Disbelievingly, Ruth stared at him, but Joseph nodded earnestly. "It's true. She's eager to have more siblings. You see, Ruthie? She had fully accepted you into our *familye*, even if she hasn't taken to calling you 'Mamm' yet. She loves you as much as she can allow herself without feeling shame."

Tears of happiness welled in Ruth's eyes as a small sob fell from her lips. She dropped her head back against Joseph's chest and he stroked her back as she cried silently.

"The *maedel* love you...and so do I," he whispered. "I can't wait to welcome our *bobbli* into this *familye* too."

The barn door opened, and a loud scoff forced the couple apart, Ruth hastily drying her eyes as David Raber frowned at them.

"I would like to go one *Chrischdaag* without encountering you two in some kind of inappropriate situation," he grumbled, but as he turned, Ruth's father appeared.

"'Ask and it shall be given you; seek and you shall find; knock and it shall be opened unto you,'" Matthew intoned, his eyes twinkling mischievously as he met his daughter's eye. "It seems to me that you keep looking for these things, David."

Grunting, he stormed off and Joseph snickered.

"I've never seen anyone get the better of my *leit* like you do, Matt," he admitted. "It's quite enjoyable to watch."

"It keeps them from hounding the *kinner*, doesn't it?"

"And they appreciate it," Joseph agreed gratefully.

It takes a village to raise a child, Ruth thought, cocking her head thoughtfully as she realized for the first time how much her father had helped in Abigail's changing attitude.

"Are you looking for us, *Daed*?" she asked sweetly.

"*Yah, komme*," Matthew called to the couple. "Everyone is sitting down to *esse* now, and the bishop is going to start with prayer."

"We need a special prayer *dienacht*," Joseph said happily. Matthew raised an eyebrow curiously.

"*Yah*? Why?"

"Because it's *Chrischdaag*," Ruth interjected smoothly, not quite ready to share in her secret with anyone other than Esther or her husband.

"It is *auld Chrischdaag* again," Matthew agreed. "And we are blessed to all be together for another year."

"You just wait to see what next year brings," Joseph laughed, leading them out of the barn and toward their waiting community.

"Only *gut* things, I hope," Matthew muttered.

"Oh, most definitely only *gut* things," Joseph promised. "This year and every other thereafter."

~*~*~

I do hope that you enjoyed reading my story.

May I suggest that you might also like to read my '*A Blessed Amish Christmas*' - *15 Book Box Set* that readers are loving!

Available on Amazon for just $0.99 or Free with Kindle Unlimited simply by clicking on the link below.

Click here to get your copy of 'A Blessed Amish Christmas - 15 Book Box Set' - Today!

Sample of Chapter One

The children had been unusually boisterous that morning, a fact that Greta could hardly fault them for. She had noticed the brilliant autumnal color changes on her way into the schoolhouse that morning, the fallen leaves gracing her walk to crunch at her feet, the crisp November air promising snow in the near future. The students were infected with the upcoming festive feeling, the knowledge that Christmas markets and celebratory plans were coming. It was perhaps a little bit too early to be making such plans, the weather was still a little too warm for such efforts, but with little eyes and little minds, they could hardly be expected to know the difference.

Still, she could not help but wish they would settle down some and heed her lessons with more attention. Greta spent so much of her evenings planning activities that would interest and keep the children engrossed. When they were not learning, she took it deeply and personally.

One child sat in the center row of the fourth-grade class, her eyes bright and clear as she tried to focus on Greta's own dark stare, even though all the others seemed more fixated on the events outside the schoolroom windows.

Finally, Greta had endured enough.

"My goodness, *kinner*," Greta chided them. "*Wat* has gotten into you all today?"

"My *vadder* said it's going to *schnee*!" Eva Byler giggled, nodding toward her brother. "Didn't he, David? Didn't he say that he could smell the *schnee* in the air?"

"He's never wrong about the first *schnee*," David agreed. "It would be a shame to miss it. We should be outside."

"How could you possibly miss it?" Greta teased them. "You'll have to walk *deheem* in it."

"You know what we mean." Eva sighed, splaying her hands over her desk. "Can't we take recess early and hope to catch the snowflakes before they fall to the ground?"

She stared pleadingly at the teacher, her youthful face full of promise and hope, neither of which Greta could easily dismiss. A part of her knew she had no business allowing such a treat but it was clear that she was not going to get anywhere with these children as they were.

With a sigh of resignation, she nodded and the children allowed a whoop of pleasure to escape their lips.

"You may take an extra ten minutes, no more," she said but her words were already falling on deaf ears.

"I want you all to bundle up," she called warningly as they flocked toward the doors. "Remember boots, hats—"

"*Yah, yah!*" they chorused, none truly listening as they rushed toward the entranceway, causing Greta to shake her blonde braid with another deep sigh. Only Nancy Sommers lingered behind, reluctant to rise and join the others as always, causing Greta to stare after her as she shuffled toward the door. The child appeared to be wasting time, as if her longer footsteps would account for the extra minutes somehow.

Greta bit on her lower lip a moment, unsure if she should do what she was considering. A part of her wanted the newcomer to make friends with the other children. She knew she should send Nancy outside to play and force the relationships that the girl appeared to fend off, but she also felt a kinship toward the outsider child. Perhaps it was the fact that Greta had always felt as if she were somewhat of an outcast herself in their small, Amish district. Growing up in Elkhart county, she had constantly been reminded that she was not as pretty as her counterparts with her "muddy" brown eyes and "stringy" blonde hair.

From a young age, Greta had recognized that she would not be courted and married off like her schoolmates, the boys regarding her more of a sister and the girls turning to her for motherly advice. It had been written in destiny that Greta would be a spinster even before her father had given up on the idea of her marrying, a fact that the girl had grown comfortable with early on.

She had always been enamored with the notion of being a schoolteacher, even if her father had been appalled by the notion at first. Ivan had attempted to talk her out of it—in the beginning.

"That is all fine and well until you're married, Greta," Ivan had protested. "But then you will have to settle down. A schoolteacher can't be married. You know that."

That had been over a decade earlier and Greta had been the longest running schoolteacher the district had seen to date. Ivan was not proud of that fact but Greta took a certain pleasure in it.

It was for this reason that she tended to single out those who needed extra attention. Those like Nancy Sommers.

"Nancy," she called out as the girl reached the doorway. Gratefully, Nancy spun around, her eyes wide and thankful. "Will you *komme* here a moment and talk with me?"

"Am I in t-t-trouble?" Nancy asked worriedly. Greta chuckled and shook her head, waving a hand to gesture the girl toward the front of the classroom.

"*Nee*, of course not," she reassured the girl. "How can you ask something like that? You've done *nix* but excellent *warrick* since the moment you arrived here. In fact, that's what I want to discuss with you."

Blinking, Nancy inched closer, wariness overtaking her face as she neared.

"Unless you would rather be *autseid* with the others. It would do you *gut* to make *freind* with the other *kinner*, you know?"

Nancy exhaled, dropping her head toward the floor, scuffing her toe along the worn, wood planks as she moved along the woodstove. The days were still warm enough that the fire did not burn at full capacity but the windows needed to be fully closed and the doors sealed to allow for the draft to be kept out.

"I don't h-h-have anything in c-common with these *kinner*," she mumbled. The answer surprised Greta and she spoke her mind freely.

"Surely they aren't that much different than those from your own district," Greta insisted. "Didn't you have friends in your own district?"

Nancy did not respond but to give a short nod—one which did not convince Greta in any way.

"You just need to give them a chance. You'll see that they're not so different than any other *kinner* you know."

A pained expression overtook Nancy's face and Greta swiftly shifted topics, sensing that she was treading on sensitive ground. She was well-aware of the terms which had brought the girl to their community and she did not wish to stir up any bad memories. Moreover, it was not why she had asked the girl to stay behind.

"Your latest essay," Greta said primly. Nancy's head jerked up in concern.

"*W-wat* about it?"

"It's *wunderbar*! I'm very impressed with how well you can write."

A tentative smile formed on Nancy's lips as she met Greta's eyes.

"*Yah?*"

"Not that I'm surprised," Greta added. "Your *warrick* has been exemplary from the moment you arrived. Your last *Lehrer* must miss you a lot. She must be wondering when you'll return to her."

Nancy blushed furiously at the compliment and again stared down at her hands, apparently tongue-tied.

"There's no reason to be embarrassed," Greta told her. "I wish you would set an example for the rest of the students. They're more interested in making snowmen than they are in learning."

Nancy laughed lightly, folding and unfolding her hands in front of her skirt.

"I'm n-not an example f-f-for anyone," she mumbled.

"I don't believe that in the least," Greta announced, shaking her head. She stepped forward and placed her hands on the younger girl's shoulders, forcing Nancy to meet her eyes directly. "It's difficult *cooma* to a new home. Your *aenti* and *onkle* appreciate the *hilf*, I'm sure. Your *vadder* must be working very hard, a lot of hours, to assist them now."

Nancy's smile faded again but before she could speak, the door opened and Henry Eicher poked his head inside.

"How much longer can we stay outside?" he asked.

"I was just *cooma* to collect you," Greta informed him. "Collect the others. It's time to resume the lessons."

He groaned lightly but did not argue, turning to retrieve his classmates as Greta offered Nancy a smile.

"I have an *iwwerfalle* for you," the teacher whispered loudly, her eyes gleaming as she ushered the girl back toward her desk. Nancy eyed her uncertainly but followed Greta's direction as the other students filed back into the single-roomed schoolhouse, shedding off their boots and coats in a din of voices.

"Settle down now," Greta called out to them. "Get into your seats."

"There was no *schnee*," Eva complained. "Can't we stay out a little longer? Just until the snow falls."

"The snow might not fall," Greta said with a sigh.

"But our *vadder* said it would and our *vadder* is never wrong!"

"Not now," Greta told her. "Maybe it will *schnee* after *schul*."

"But I can smell it in the air!" Eva insisted.

"It won't go anywhere." Greta sighed. "Anyway, I have a special surprise for you."

Her words silenced the group, all eyes turning to her with interest.

"It isn't very often that I am blessed with *warrick* so moving, so delightful, that I think it should be shared with everyone," Greta explained, nodding toward Nancy. "Nancy, will you *komme* here for a moment, *pliese?*"

Nancy paled where she sat, shaking her head.

"*N-nee…*" she squeaked but Greta insisted.

"*Komme,*" she said, extending her hand. "We're all *freind* here. There's no reason to be afraid."

The children began to murmur amongst themselves, confused by this latest turn of events and Greta shuffled toward her desk, retrieving Nancy's essay with a beam.

"This is what I want all of you to aspire toward," she told the group, holding up the pages. "This is how one should write from the heart and with such poise. I want you to listen to Nancy's words and hear how they ring true, *yah?*"

Nancy stood, shaking, at the head of the classroom as Greta joined her side, handing the essay to the girl.

"Go on, Nancy. Read it to them."

"*N-nee*, I don't w-want to," Nancy whimpered.

"It's all right, *liebling*. There's *nix* to fear here. Go on. I'm right here beside you."

She smiled encouragingly and Nancy's face turned opaque. Desperately, she looked around the building, the children's eyes fixated on her expectantly.

"Go on," Greta urged. "You should be proud, not embarrassed. Go ahead and read what you have written."

The children began to giggle amongst themselves, casting the new girl amused glances. Greta looked at them sternly but when she turned back to Nancy, there was fire in the child's face.

"*N-nee!*" Nancy howled, grabbing the pages from Greta's hands. "I s-s-said I don't w-w-want to!"

With that, the girl scampered toward the door, her coat forsaken as she rushed into the cool afternoon air, leaving Greta to gape after her in horror and confusion.

"Nancy!" Greta choked, hurrying toward the door but she had moved too slowly. The girl was halfway across the field by the time Greta approached the schoolhouse steps, showing no signs of returning. With a heavy heart, she turned back to her students, stunned and humiliated at what she had done.

"I can read my essay," Eva chirped. "But only if you let us go outside too!"

"Open your writing books." Greta frowned, her words barely rasps as she closed the door to block the chilled air. Shame overcame her as she realized that she had embarrassed the girl in a way that she had vowed never to do to a child.

I will make it right with Nancy, she promised, blinking away tears of contrition. *I will get her to trust me again.*

Click here to get your copy of 'A Blessed Amish Christmas - 15 Book Box Set' - Today!

A NOTE FROM THE AUTHOR

Dear Reader,

I do hope that you enjoyed reading '**The Amish Christmas Storm**'

Possibly you even identify with the characters in some small way. Many of us presume to know God's will for our lives, and don't realize that His timing often does not match our own.

The foremost reason that I love writing about the Amish is that their lifestyle is diametrically opposed to the Western norm. The simplicity and purity evident there is so vastly refreshing that the story lines derived from them are suitable for everyone.

Be sure to keep an eye out for the next book which is coming soon.

Emma Cartwright

∼

Thank You!

Thank you for purchasing this book. We hope that you have enjoyed reading it.

If you enjoyed reading this book **please may you consider leaving a review** — it really would help greatly to get the word out!

∾

Newsletter

If you love reading sweet, clean, Amish Romance stories why not join Emma Cartwright's newsletter and receive advance notification of new releases and more!

Simply sign up here: http://eepurl.com/dgw2I5

And get your *FREE* copy of **Amish Unexpected Love**

∾

Contact Me

If you'd simply like to drop us a line you can contact us at **emma@emmacartwrightbooks.com**

You can also connect with me on my new **Facebook page**.

I will always let you know about new releases on my Facebook page, so it is worth liking that if you get the chance.

LIKE EMMA'S FB PAGE HERE

I welcome your thoughts and would love to hear from you!

I will then also be able to let you know about new books coming out along with Amazon special deals etc

Made in the USA
Columbia, SC
15 January 2024